Death & Due Diligence

A Paradox Murder Mystery

Book Seven

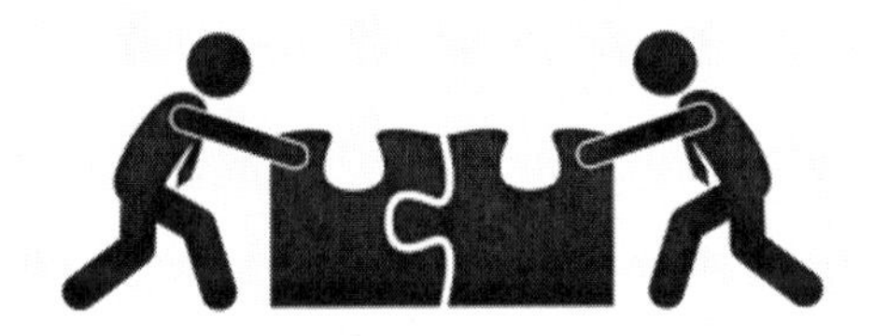

Death & Due Diligence

A Paradox Murder Mystery

Book Seven

Charles J Thayer

Death & Due Diligence

By

Charles J Thayer

Chartwell Publications
Palm City, Florida

ISBN: 9798402448384

This story is a work of fiction.

The locations and many of the associated people in Boothbay Harbor are real. Other characters and events are all fictitious and only exist in the author's imagination. Any resemblance to actual people, living or dead, and events is entirely coincidental and unintentional.

Dedication

Global Coronavirus Pandemic

Death & Due Diligence is dedicated to all the essential service workers who continue to risk their health by going to work every day during our ongoing global pandemic.

Health care professionals, law enforcement officers, grocery store clerks, drug store staff, mail carriers, truck drivers, delivery personnel, teachers, bank tellers, and all the others who are out there every day doing their jobs.

The media is right; you are heroes!

Thank You – Please Stay Safe

"Trust but Verify"

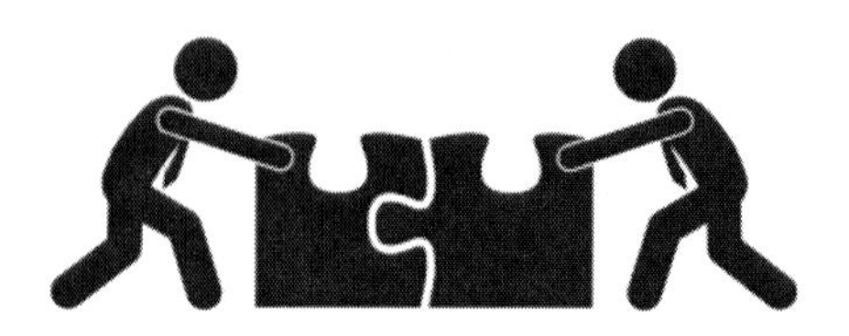

Due Diligence: The investigation and verification of financial, operational, and legal representations before entering a business transaction.

Prologue

My name is Steve Wilson. Five years ago, I was Chief Auditor at one of our nation's largest banks headquartered in New York City. After thirty-five years of corporate life, I elected to take early retirement at age fifty-five.

I've always enjoyed the challenge of solving financial crimes. After my retirement, I founded Paradox-Research to investigate fraud and money laundering. I didn't expect to solve murders.

Amanda Smith and I first crossed paths during a murder investigation in Maine. Today, she's an FBI Agent and we frequently team up to investigate financial crime.

My readers know I enjoy my new freedom from corporate life and prefer to work, write and travel aboard Paradox, my custom-designed, Maine-built, lobster boat.

Welcome aboard,

Steve

Paradox09A@Gmail.com
[09A: Crime Code for Murder]

1

Boothbay Harbor, Maine
Friday Morning - June, 2021

"Daddy, why isn't that man swimming?"

"What man, honey?"

"That man. Over there."

"Oh, shit!"

"That's a bad word, daddy."

"Honey, you need to go down in the salon with mommy."

"Nancy! Take Mindy down to the salon and call the Harbormaster. We have an emergency!"

Nancy's head pops out of their sailboat's hatch. "What's wrong?"

"There. I'm going over in our dinghy."

"My God! He's not moving. Mindy, stop staring! Come with me."

Nancy takes Mindy's hand, leads her down the steps into the salon, and grabs the VHF radio mike above the sailboat's navigation desk.

"Boothbay Harbormaster! Boothbay Harbormaster! This is the sailing yacht Adventure on mooring #22. We have a medical emergency. Please hurry!"

"This is the Harbormaster. What's the nature of your medical emergency?"

"A motionless man is floating in the harbor. My husband's going out in our dinghy to help."

"I'm on my way!"

2

"Hey Kim, thanks for helping with my lines. It's great to be back at Boothbay Harbor."

"Welcome back! Paradox looks fresh out of the box. How was your voyage down from Belfast?"

Paradox at Boothbay Harbor Marina

"Justin and his crew always have Paradox looking like new when she's waiting at the dock at Front Street Shipyard. It only took me a few days to get settled and provision at Hannaford's supermarket. The fog on Penobscot Bay dissipated early this morning. I had a pleasant five-hour run on a calm, sunny day. It'll take less than an hour to wash the sea salt off her decks."

"When's Amanda coming?"

"She's working at the FBI's New York office and

won't be free until the July 4th weekend."

"I thought she was working from Portland."

"Mark Bouchard, the director of the Financial Crimes Division in New York, authorized fully vaccinated staff to return to his office in the city and travel on assignments."

I ask, "What's all the activity out in the harbor?"

"I don't know. I'm waiting for Jeff to swing by this afternoon. He received a call on the VHF radio early this morning about an emergency. The Coast Guard, Marine Patrol, and State Police all converged on a sailboat after he arrived."

"Sounds serious. No chatter on the marine radio?"

"No. He must have called them on his cell phone."

I gesture over Kim's shoulder. "Hey! Here he comes. This morning's crisis must be over."

Boothbay Harbor Harbormaster

Kim takes Jeff's spring line as he glides to the marina's floating dock. I grab the stern line and he shouts, "Hey Steve, welcome back!"

"Thanks! Looks like you had a busy morning."

"Wicked early morning and I'm starved. I need to pick up a sandwich at Red Cup."

"I'll join you. Just arrived and I'm ready for an afternoon coffee and something to eat."

Kim frowns. "Not so fast! What's all the activity?"

Jeff glances back at Kim as we walk down the dock. "I'll update you when we return."

I shake my head as we approach the ramp up from the marina's floating dock. "Damn. Low tide again. It takes weeks for me to adjust to these ten-foot tides. Climbing these steep ramps is tough."

We cross Pier One to join a dozen customers waiting to order at Red Cup's takeout window.

Jeff asks, "How's Amanda?"

"She's great and busy with her job in New York. She won't have time to join me until July 4th."

"Too bad. She always brightens up the waterfront." Jeff continues, "How was your winter? Rumor has it you guys were in Florida."

"The rumor is accurate. I thought we might spend time on Paradox, but one of Amanda's assignments required a change of plans. You can read about it in *Prospère Puzzle*, my new book. Sherman's Book Shop is planning a book signing event."

"Did you bring Paradox back up the Intracoastal?"

"No. Shipped her by truck to Front Street Shipyard and flew into Bangor. I returned the rental car in Belfast after organizing my gear and provisioning. It was an easy cruise down Penobscot Bay and along the coast after the fog lifted this morning."

Jeff says, "You first," as we reach the window.

Dan greets me with a smile. "Hey, Steve. Welcome back! Ready for your regular afternoon latte?"

"Thanks, Dan. It's good to be back. I'm starved and would like one of your BLTs with my latte."

"Good to see you. Stop back when we're not so busy." Dan turns to Jeff.

Jeff says, "Please, add a coffee to my BLT and Steve's coffee is on me today."

Dan laughs. "Save your money. Steve's latte is on the house today. He has credits from last summer. Your orders will be at the pickup window."

Boothbay Harbor Public Landing

The Red Cup's service is quick, and we walk across

the street to the Public Landing.

I ask, "Want to stop at a picnic table to eat?"

Jeff shakes his head. "Not a chance. Kim will kill me if we don't go back to the marina."

Kim is standing with hands on her hips by the marina's red picnic table as we step carefully down the steep ramp. "OK, Jeff, what's the story? I heard the emergency call this morning, but you guys went off the air."

Jeff and I both sit at the table with our sandwiches while Kim remains standing and staring at Jeff.

He takes a sip of coffee. "A family from Virginia rented a mooring a couple of days ago to view the Tall Ships and enjoy Windjammer Days. It was still foggy this morning, but their little girl spotted a body floating in the water. Her father launched their dinghy to investigate and her mother called me."

Kim frowns. "That's awful. What happened?"

"Damned if I know. The guy's life jacket was inflated, but he was unresponsive. The medical crew said he died hours before we arrived."

I ask, "Were you able to identify the victim?"

"The name of a boat was stenciled on his life jacket and the police found a wallet in his trousers. His dinghy was tied to the boarding ladder of his sailboat. We assume he slipped while trying to board. Guess he couldn't climb back aboard and he passed out in the cold water and drowned. I wanted to keep his death off the marine radio with visitors coming for Windjammer Days."

Kim asks, "Was he local?"

"Sorry. That's all they'll let me say today. The state police took charge, a forensic team showed up, and took a bunch of samples and photos. The officers asked the family who discovered the body a lot of questions."

"You were out there all morning." Kim frowns. "That's all you know?"

"Sorry, that's all they'll let me say today, but I'm sure forensics will welcome your help," Jeff chides Kim.

He turns to me. "What are your plans for the summer?"

"We plan to keep Paradox at Kim's marina as our home base again. Boothbay Harbor is a little over an hour from Portland, but our weekends require more planning with Amanda working in New York."

Jeff gives me a quizzical look. "How do you feel about that?"

"Yogi Berra had it right. It's 'Déjà vu all over again'. I worked twelve-hour days during my banking career. Amanda loves her new job, so it's her turn to work long hours. I keep busy with my banking clients and writing murder mysteries."

Jeff shrugs. "Good luck. She's a keeper. I gotta get back. Lots of boats coming in for the lobster boat races tomorrow. It's crazy with the Tall Ships and

Windjammer Days starting this weekend."

Kim hands Jeff his dock lines and grins. "You better have more to say tomorrow morning if you expect a fresh cup of coffee."

# # #

Friday evening finds me checking email and reviewing this week's investment performance after washing the salt spray off Paradox. It's still light at eight-thirty when I grill a steak and move my folding teak table out to the aft deck for dinner.

Amanda calls at ten. "Thanks for texting. I breathe easier when you're safe after moving Paradox by yourself. How's Kim and what's happening in Boothbay?"

"Cheerful, as always. Kim makes everyone feel special. It's good to be back. I also had a BLT from Red Cup and a brief visit with Jeff this afternoon. Kim's marina feels like home. How soon can you join me for a weekend?"

"I won't be returning to New York from Seattle until next week. I'm joining my investigation team for dinner in a few minutes. Don't worry, I've blocked off time for the July 4th weekend. You keeping busy?"

"Yes, but no new assignments and no travel planned until mid-July. I'm looking forward to the lobster boat races tomorrow. I'll miss you."

"Miss you too. Gotta go, I'll try to call tomorrow."

3

The typical Saturday morning line is waiting on the sidewalk to order breakfast at Red Cup. Dan greets me when it's my turn. "Morning, Steve! You want to start your day with another free latte you carried over from last summer? You have two more saved on your account."

"No. Happy to pay. I don't need an incentive to visit. I also want to start my summer with one of your delicious raspberry bars."

Schooners at Public Landing

The sun feels warm on my face when I stop at the Public Landing. I set my latte on the railing and devour my raspberry bar while admiring the two schooners being prepped at the town dock for public tours during Windjammer Week. I take a deep breath when I finish my bar. It's relaxing to return to my morning routine in Boothbay, and I continue my short walk back to Kim's marina.

I'm finishing the coffee on my aft deck when I hear Jeff stop on his morning rounds.

The red picnic table next to Kim's dock office is news central for the marina. I hear Jeff ask, "Any coffee?" as I step to the dock to join the conversation.

Kim grins. "Depends on your morning news."

"The state police called for an investigation and the state is sending an investigator."

"Why?"

He smiles and hands her his mug. "Isn't that sufficient for a top-up on my morning coffee?"

Kim shrugs. "I guess. I just brewed a fresh pot."

She returns with Jeff's mug. "Ok. Why the state investigator?"

"Just a precaution. The guy's swim ladder was down and we're all curious why he wasn't able to climb aboard. The police are waiting on the state medical examiner to determine the cause of death. It will take at least a week for the official report, so don't harass me. I'll let you know."

Jeff turns to me. "You taking Paradox out to watch the lobster boat races today?"

"No. I want to avoid the crazy spectator traffic and

plan to take my binoculars and handheld marine radio with me for lunch on Tugboat Inn's rooftop restaurant. I'll have a great view of the races and can follow the results."

"Good idea. I'll be busy keeping careless spectators out of the racecourse. Common sense is not very common on race day." He turns to Kim. "Thanks for the refill."

# # #

Amanda calls late afternoon. "Sorry, I didn't have time to talk last night. I plan to turn this case over to our attorneys next week and we were discussing legal strategy. We'll finalize the evidence this weekend so I can return to New York. Did you watch the races?"

Lobster Boat Race @ Boothbay Register

"Yes. I even recognized some boats. You will be happy to know Heather Thompson on Gold Digger won her class."

Amanda says, "Wonderful! Great to see a woman compete."

I continue. "It was enlightening to visit with a couple onboard their boat last night at Kim's marina. Their boat sure looks like a traditional working lobster boat, but it's built out of carbon fiber and the diesel engine produces over a thousand horsepower. Their boat hits fifty miles an hour and won its class today."

"It sounds too fancy to be a working lobster boat. Do they really pull traps?"

"Not full-time. He has an office job and qualifies for the races with a license for personal consumption. Interesting couple, and they race for fun."

Amanda laughs. "The races only pay a few dollars in prize money. It's all about small trophies and bragging rights. How busy is Boothbay?"

I say, "It's crazy. The Santa Maria came into the marina for Tall Ships today and we have two schooners down at Public Landing. Lots of people on the docks for the public tours and I see out-of-state tags again."

Amanda says, "Last summer was rough with all the Covid restrictions. It's nice to know visitors are returning."

"I hope you're still joining me for July 4th."

"Absolutely! Already purchased my ticket and I'll drive to Boothbay after I arrive in Portland Thursday afternoon. I need to return to New York Tuesday morning on the six o'clock flight. That's the best I could do given my caseload."

4

I'm reading the online edition of the New York Sunday Times on my boat's aft deck when my phone flashes *unknown number*. A beep announces a message.

I suspect another robocall to renew the warranty on my non-existent car, but place my coffee on the table and touch the message icon on my phone.

Hi, this is Brian Tucker. I hope you remember me. I managed the New York bank's capital markets division. Sorry to bother you on a Sunday morning. It's important. Please call me today.

Humm .... I remember Brian as an excellent manager and our audits of capital markets were uneventful. I'm curious why he's calling on a Sunday morning and return his call.

Brian answers. "Wow! Thanks for being so prompt. I wasn't sure you would remember me."

"No problem. Are you still at the bank?"

"No. I joined an investment banking firm a couple of years after you retired. We're working on a complex acquisition and encountered an unexpected problem. I hope you can help me with a due diligence assignment."

I pause. "Maybe. Why me?"

"As I remember, you managed due diligence for all the New York bank's acquisitions. We need help from someone with your experience."

"What do you have in mind?"

"As you know, investment bankers use code names for acquisition negotiations. We call our client Tango. It's a technology company that received a confidential inquiry about acquiring Beta, another technology company owned by Alpha, a private equity firm. Tango's board held an emergency meeting this morning, and the CEO asked me to contact you."

"Emergency meeting?"

"We're engaged in mutual due diligence. John Michaud, a retired partner from Tango's accounting firm, was conducting due diligence for us."

"So. What's the emergency?"

"Michaud died in a tragic accident a few days ago and we are under time pressure to announce the transaction."

"Why can't the accounting firm assign another partner to complete due diligence?"

"It's a regional firm, and this retired senior partner was the only person with the appropriate level of independence and due diligence experience. That's why I'm calling you."

"What would you like me to do?"

"We want you to complete our due diligence."

"Thanks for the confidence, but I'm not sure a technology acquisition fits my skill-set."

Brian says, "The New York bank operated on a variety of complex technology platforms. You have more than adequate technology knowledge and audit experience for this assignment."

I pause before continuing. "Maybe. What can you tell me about the transaction?"

"Nothing more until you sign a non-disclosure agreement. We have an expert evaluating the technology. We need you to verify Beta's financial reports."

I ask, "When's the report due?"

"Alpha's pushing to complete due diligence by the end of this week. I told them, given the circumstances, we need at least two weeks. Alpha agreed to wait until the July 4th weekend to complete due diligence and we plan to announce Tango's purchase of Beta before the market opens on Tuesday, July 6th. Do you have time to do this?"

"I might have time before the holiday to complete a report. That's not much time and I won't issue a report until I'm satisfied with my analysis. Send me your NDA so I can evaluate the project and see if completing my financial due diligence report in two weeks is feasible."

Brian says, "I just emailed the NDA to you at Paradox-Research. Please get back to me as soon as possible."

"Give me a couple of hours."

# # #

As expected, the NDA discloses the names of the firms engaged in the acquisition discussions. Tango is a public company listed on the New York Stock Exchange and public documents provide a wealth of information. Alpha and Beta are both private firms and I only find limited information online.

My first challenge is deciphering the descriptions of Tango and Beta. Tango's shareholder reports say:

Tango provides technology solutions that optimize and accelerate manufacturing processes with custom technology platforms and services that empower our client's businesses around the world. Tango's strong and dedicated technology teams support our clients in all major global markets.

Beta's CEO, Max Miller, posts frequent press releases on Beta's website describing his success:

Beta's fantastic turnaround has transformed the company into the fastest growing provider of fully integrated, end-to-end technology solutions for our global clients.

A brief article in a national financial publication about 'Magic Max' Miller's aggressive management style is not complementary.

When I finish my research, I email Sarah, my research analyst, and walk across the nearby footbridge to contemplate the challenge of completing our due diligence report in two weeks.

I return to my boat with mixed feelings. Sarah emailed she is available to assist me and I call Brian. "I've signed your NDA on behalf of my firm, Paradox-Research. I've disclosed the timing of the report to my research analyst, and she will assist me if we decide to accept your assignment. But first, I need to ask you a few questions."

"Fire away. What do you want to know?"

"What do Tango and Beta do? The 'buzz words' in their corporate descriptions sound sophisticated, but they don't say a damn thing."

Brian laughs. "The investor relations people craft these descriptions to attract investors. I agree, it's useless cocktail party talk. I doubt many investors understand either business, they just look at the financial results."

"So, what do Tango and Beta do? Why is this a profitable match? What should I investigate?"

"Both firms buy computer chips made in Taiwan. They both outsource assembly of specialized circuit boards with custom software designed to control production equipment used by manufacturing firms. Tango contracts for assembly in Singapore and Beta outsources with several outfits in China. Both firms have global sales and service teams to support their customers. They offer similar products and support services, but they have little customer and product overlap. The purchase of Beta will expand Tango's menu of products and services to domestic and international clients."

He adds, "We hired an independent technology analyst to evaluate Beta's software and products.

Her report says Beta's existing technology is solid, but they have nothing new in their pipeline. Tango's research teams constantly work with their customers to develop new custom software, so the post-acquisition plan delivers Tango's new products to Beta's customers."

I ask, "What about Beta's supply chains? Hasn't Covid disrupted chip supplies from Taiwan and assembly in China?"

"Our technology analyst is preparing a detailed analysis of Beta's chip availability and assembly capacity. We only want you to verify Beta's financial results."

"I'm concerned by this short two-week deadline, but I have a personal incentive to finish by July 4th. Is the financial data I need already on your secure data site? Have Alpha and Beta both been fully cooperative?"

Brian hesitates. "I'm not sure. Michaud was requesting some additional information. I don't know the status of his request."

"Do you know what he was requesting?"

"Michaud copied me on his emails to Patrick O'Donnell, Alpha's CFO. He requested additional detail on foreign sales a few days before his accident."

"Do you know why?"

"No. We planned to talk after he received the information and he completed his report."

"I need face-to-face meetings with O'Donnell and Miller. I want a private meeting with Earl Baxter, the partner in charge of their independent audits."

Brian says, "Everyone will cooperate. I'll arrange your meetings and email your data requests to O'Donnell." He pauses. "Have you signed our engagement letter?"

"Not yet. What happens if I'm not finished in two weeks?"

"We will both have to deal with some very unhappy people. Everyone wants this deal to happen."

"Humm .... Will Tango close at any cost?"

Brian bristles. "Of course not! That's why you're doing due diligence. We agreed in principle to pay twenty times the past twelve months' earnings. We want you to verify Beta's earnings."

"That clarifies my assignment. I'm emailing you a signed copy of my firm's engagement agreement. I've also attached our due diligence checklist. We can discuss next steps once Tango approves my engagement and I've cross-referenced our list with Beta's financial information on your data site."

"Great! Thank you. I need to review your engagement letter with Vince Parker, Tango's CEO, and our attorneys. I'll set up a call with them tonight and confirm your engagement first thing Monday morning."

# # #

Amanda calls at eleven Sunday night. "This time

zone difference is awkward. I'm getting ready for dinner and you're probably ready for bed."

"No worries. I'm happy to talk anytime."

She says, "My team's had a productive weekend and I'm headed back to New York Tuesday. Sorry to be so preoccupied with work. My caseload looks manageable for the next two weeks and I'm looking forward to seeing you over the July 4th weekend. How are you?"

"Looks like I might be busy the next two weeks helping with a due diligence assignment. They want my report finished before the end of the month, so we can still enjoy the holiday together."

She sighs. "Love you. You better be finished. I'm ready for a break."

5

"Good morning, Steve. I hope eight isn't too early on a Monday morning. Parker approved your engagement and I'm texting you the address and password for our online data site. Parker wants to set up a conference call at eleven."

"Thanks. That works for me. What more can you tell me about these negotiations?"

Brian replies, "Tango is headquartered in Boston, and Alpha, the private equity firm, is also based in Boston. Carson Fullerton, Alpha's chairman, called Vince Parker, Tango's CEO in early May to arrange dinner. Fullerton proposed to sell Beta to Tango for a mix of cash and stock."

"Humm ...... Fullerton initiated contact and wants to sell. Why does Parker want to buy Beta?"

"Beta sells complementary products. So, Parker can offer Beta's products to Tango's customers and he can offer his products to Beta's customers. In addition, Beta's international sales growth will expand Tango's foreign business. We believe an acquisition at twenty times Beta's earnings will produce a significant increase in the value of Tango's stock."

"Is that why Fullerton suggested a deal for cash and stock?"

"Yes. Fullerton wants his investors to benefit from the expected increase in Tango's stock price. Tango is larger than Beta, so Beta's sales will only represent one-fourth of the combined company. Fullerton proposed a transaction for sixty percent cash and forty percent stock. Alpha will become one of Tango's largest shareholders with a ten percent ownership. Miller, Beta's CEO, will resign after the acquisition, and Vince Parker and Tango's management team will manage the combined business. You'll find a diagram of the proposed transaction on our data site."

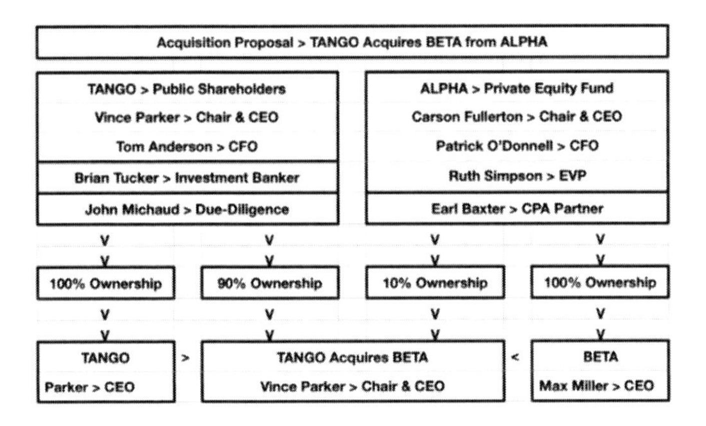

Brian continues. "The cash Alpha receives will repay the bank loans used to buy Beta. Fullerton expects Tango's stock price to increase significantly after the acquisition and he'll look like a hero to his investors. Everyone is excited about the prospects for the combined companies. Patrick O'Donnell, Alpha's CFO, downloaded electronic versions of Beta's financial reports to our data site and Michaud started our due diligence two weeks ago."

I ask. "How much progress did Michaud make before his accident?"

Brian hesitates. "I'm not sure. Alpha has offices in Boston and West Palm Beach. Fullerton's office is in Boston, but he is spending the summer working from his yacht in Maine. O'Donnell's office and Beta's headquarters are both in West Palm. I arranged two face-to-face due diligence meetings with O'Donnell, Max Miller, and Earl Baxter in Palm Beach. Tango's accounting firm is looking for Michaud's notes and a copy of his draft report."

"I need to review the information on your data site before our call with Parker. I'll prepare a list of any additional information I need and you can schedule my meetings."

# # #

I pour a cup of coffee, open my laptop, and start reviewing the information on Brian's secure site.

At ten o'clock, I call Brian. "We have a problem to discuss before our conference call with Parker."

Brian responds. "Shit! What's the problem?"

"I can't verify Beta's financial results with the limited information O'Donnell has provided. He's only posted summary management reports for Beta. He hasn't produced the detailed monthly financial reports Michaud requested. I've emailed you an updated document request."

Brian ponders. "This seems like a lot of information to provide in such a short time. We don't want to be unreasonable."

"It's the same information Michaud requested. Fullerton can't monitor Beta's performance without this information. O'Donnell must have everything Michaud requested as part of Beta's monthly financial reports. No reason he can't post those reports to your data site today."

Brian asks, "Why are you requesting financial information from Alpha? Tango will buy Beta. We're not buying Fullerton's private equity fund."

"Beta's annual audit for Alpha's investors refers to extensive intercompany transactions between Fullerton's fund and Beta. We need to understand those transactions."

"When do you want to schedule your meetings with management?"

"Let's start with O'Donnell and Miller. I want to understand Beta's operations and financial results before I meet with Parker."

"I'll ask O'Donnell, but we might get pushback."

"Tango is buying Beta and we need to verify Beta's financial information. Mutual due diligence requires a mutual sharing of information."

Brian sighs. "OK. I called him this morning to say we hired you to complete our due diligence. I'll email your data request."

I ask, "When do you expect to post a copy of Michaud's due diligence files?"

"Not sure. No due diligence files were in his office, at his home, or on his boat. The managing partner suspects they may have been lost in Michaud's accident."

"Humm …….. Michaud didn't post any notes or analysis to your data site. Did he discuss his analysis with you?"

"No. He didn't discuss his report with me or his firm's senior partner. Michaud said he wanted to remain independent and didn't want to discuss his report until it was complete."

\# # #

Brian calls me at eleven and the first voice I hear says, "Good morning, Steve. This is Vince Parker. Brian shared your background with our board and I'm pleased you accepted our due diligence assignment. Carson Fullerton is pushing for an announcement in two weeks, but I want you to do a thorough job. I don't want to see a boiler-plate report just to get Fullerton's deal across the finish line."

"What if I uncover a problem?"

"I don't expect you will, but if you do, I want to know about it. I'm not doing this deal at any cost."

\# # #

Brian calls at nine Monday evening. "Sorry to call so late. I emailed your list to O'Donnell after we spoke, but he didn't respond until this evening. He discussed your request with Miller and said Fullerton wants to have lunch with you tomorrow."

"Interesting. Where does he want to meet?"

"Fullerton's on his yacht and said you can meet him for lunch tomorrow in Camden, Maine. Can you travel to Camden on such short notice?"

"Not a problem. I'm working from my boat in Maine and can rent a car to drive to Camden for lunch. Just let me know the time and place."

"The name of Fullerton's yacht is *Private Equity*. O'Donnell said to meet Fullerton at noon for lunch aboard the yacht at the Lyman-Morse marina."

# # #

"Kim, I need help. I just scheduled lunch in Camden for tomorrow, and no rental cars are available on short notice. Any ideas?"

"Give me an hour. I'll see what I can do."

I'm on my aft deck with my laptop when Kim approaches. "I've located a local college student who can drive you tomorrow. Emma is home for the summer and works evenings at a restaurant, so she needs to be back by five."

"No worries. We should be back well before five. I'll certainly compensate her."

6

Camden, Maine

I change from blue jeans and a nautical t-shirt to a yellow polo with khakis and blue blazer for lunch. Emma meets me at ten Tuesday morning in her red Ford pickup for our one-hour drive to Camden. We arrive in time for coffee at the Owl & Turtle Bookstore before she drops me off across the harbor at Lyman-Morse at ten minutes to twelve.

Fullerton's yacht is on the face dock and I shout up to a young woman wearing a white monogrammed polo with khaki shorts. "Good morning. My name is Steve Wilson. I have a lunch appointment with Carson Fullerton."

Ten minutes later, a large muscular man dressed in a tight black t-shirt, a black facemask, and black pants descends the yacht's stainless-steel stairs to the dock. "Show me your identification and proof of Covid vaccination."

"Sure. Brian told me you would ask."

"Wait on the dock."

I'm pacing the dock when the man in black reappears twenty minutes later and says, "Come aboard." He leads me to an empty table with six deck chairs on the aft deck. "Mr. Fullerton will join you shortly."

I pull out a chair, and the young woman appears ten minutes later. "May I serve you a cocktail?"

"Thanks. Not for lunch. Ice tea will be fine."

I'm on my second glass of ice tea when a slightly overweight man in a blue polo and khakis walks out of the salon door at one o'clock. "So, you're the accountant asking for my private information. Why is that necessary?"

I stand and extend my hand. "I assume you're Carson Fullerton. My name is Steve Wilson. It's nice to meet you."

Fullerton ignores my extended hand and folds his arms across his chest. I withdraw my hand and we face each other eye-to-eye.

I say, "This isn't your first acquisition negotiation and you know mutual due diligence requires both parties to share information. We've done our part. It's your turn to share the information we've requested if you expect this transaction to be announced in two weeks."

"This intrusive request for information about my private equity fund is unnecessary. The transaction is between Tango and Beta."

"You would ask for the same information if you were in my position. Beta's financial footnotes refer to intercompany transactions with Alpha. I need to understand these intercompany relationships to issue my due diligence report."

Fullerton raises his voice. "That's bullshit. I'm authorizing you to issue your report without Alpha's information and we will announce the acquisition as planned."

I lower my voice. "Mr. Fullerton, it's not necessary to make a standard due diligence request difficult. I don't work for you. I work for the management and board of directors of Tango. I suggest you arrange the meetings I requested and instruct your CFO to cooperate."

"We'll see about that." I'm left standing on the aft deck, watching his abrupt departure into the salon.

A minute later, the man in black appears and says, "I'll escort you off the yacht."

# # #

Emma is waiting in the marina's parking lot. "That's a fancy yacht. How was lunch?"

"Well, my meeting was interesting. We didn't have lunch and I'm hungry. If it's OK with you, let's drive around the harbor to a waterfront café."

My phone flashes a call from Brian before I have time to look at the menu. I answer, "Hold on," and look at Emma. "I need to take this call. Please excuse me and order me a fish sandwich when our server returns. Order anything you want. Thanks."

I walk to a vacant spot on the railing overlooking Camden's harbor. "I can talk now."

"What happened at lunch? O'Donnell says we need to replace you."

"It was a brief conversation and lunch was not on the agenda. Fullerton kept me waiting for an hour. He refused to provide Alpha's financial information. I said he needed to arrange the meetings and information we requested for me to issue my report to Tango." I pause. "It was a strange meeting. Have you talked with Fullerton?"

"No. I've never met or talked to Fullerton. He doesn't negotiate with investment bankers. All my discussions are with O'Donnell, but Fullerton is the decision maker."

"Humm ..... That's his approach. Fullerton stays in the background like the Wizard of Oz and plays puppet master with his CFO. Doesn't that make it difficult for you to negotiate a transaction?"

"Yes, but that's what I get paid to do."

"What did you tell O'Donnell? Am I fired?"

"I told him we need the information you requested if he wants the acquisition announced on schedule. He wasn't happy, but said he would talk to Fullerton."

Fullerton's attitude piques my curiosity and, before returning to the table, I email Sarah, asking her to call me.

Sarah is a fictitious name for a young woman I encountered during my banking career. She risked her life by cooperating with me during a foreign fraud investigation, and the FBI granted her immunity for her testimony. Sarah is a talented programmer and Mark arranged a new identity for her in the witness protection program. She helps me with research, and we use an encrypted email account at Paradox-Research. I don't know her new identity, and she disguises her phone number with the name of a famous artist when she calls or sends me a text.

I see *Picasso* flash on my iPhone just as my haddock sandwich arrives. Emma smiles. "I've had lunch. I'll give you privacy so you can eat," and she walks over to the railing to view the boats.

I say, "Hi. Thanks for your prompt reply."

"No problem. It's a convenient time. How was lunch?"

"Not sure. Fullerton doesn't want to share all the information we requested and wants me fired."

"That doesn't sound like a good start. What does he have to hide?"

"That's the question. For openers, please run a background check on Carson Fullerton and his CFO, Patrick O'Donnell."

# # #

Emma drops me off in front of Sherman's bookstore at four. "Sorry, this took longer than expected. Here's a little extra for your time and patience."

She smiles. "Thanks. I don't think you had a very good day. You hardly said a word on our drive back to Boothbay."

"You're perceptive. I've had better days."

# # #

I'm browsing articles on Bloomberg about Alpha when I receive a call from Brian Tuesday evening.

"O'Donnell called and said he will meet you at Alpha's offices in Palm Beach on Thursday. A limo will pick you up in Boothbay at eleven tomorrow and you will fly to Palm Beach on Fullerton's private jet. O'Donnell said Ruth Simpson will call you tomorrow morning to confirm arrangements."

"Then Fullerton agreed to cooperate?"

"Not entirely. O'Donnell said you can review the additional financial and sales reports you requested on their accounting system at his office, but he will not post any new confidential information on our due diligence site. Is that satisfactory?"

"It's a start. Let's talk again tomorrow morning before I head to Palm Beach."

# # #

Amanda calls me later Tuesday night. "I'm at the airport and will be on the red-eye tonight back to New York. Our lawyers expect to file charges in a few days. How was your lunch on the yacht?"

"My so-called lunch invitation was weird. The yacht's owner was arrogant. He kept me waiting for an hour. Lunch was not served, and he told my client to fire me."

"Whoa! What happened?"

"That's all I can say at the moment. I'm not fired

and a limo will pick me up tomorrow for a flight on a private jet to Palm Beach. This simple assignment is looking a little more challenging than I expected."

"A private jet sounds better than my coach seat on a red-eye tonight. Sorry, I gotta go, the flight's boarding. Talk to you tomorrow. Love you."

"Love you, too."

7

Wednesday morning, I risk answering the call when my phone flashes *unknown number*.

"Good morning, Steve. This is Ruth Simpson. I hope seven-thirty isn't too early. Carson's Rolls will pick you up at eleven. Where do you want to meet Carson's driver?"

"I'll meet him in front of Sherman's bookstore. It's on Commercial Street along Boothbay Harbor's waterfront."

"Carson's driver will recognize you. I will meet you at the private aircraft terminal in Portland for our flight to Palm Beach."

# # #

I call Brian on my walk to Red Cup for my morning latte. "Ruth Simpson just called to confirm arrangements. She was very cordial. I'm surprised at the change in attitude. Curious to see how helpful O'Donnell will be. Can you give me a little more background on this deal?"

"Sure. Fullerton offered to sell Beta for twenty-five times earnings at their dinner. Parker viewed that price as excessive, but he hired our firm to analyze the benefits of combining the two firms."

"Have there been any additional meetings between Fullerton and Parker?"

"No. In mid-May, I met O'Donnell in Palm Beach and proposed a transaction at twenty times earnings."

"What was his response?"

"He didn't expect a positive response from Miller or Fullerton. We were surprised when O'Donnell emailed me a draft acquisition agreement with the price calculated at twenty times earnings. Your job is to verify Beta's earnings before I negotiate their other proposed deal points."

"Why are they in a rush to announce a deal?"

"Fullerton wants to announce the transaction before any leaks occur that influence Tango's stock price. If Tango's stock price goes up before the announcement, then Alpha gets fewer shares."

"What do you know about O'Donnell?"

"He's Alpha's contact person and negotiator. But he isn't the decision maker. Every single deal point needs to be approved by Fullerton. O'Donnell has a reputation as a clever financial architect and Fullerton hired him to structure Alpha's investment transactions."

"What do you know about Max Miller, Beta's CEO?"

"Only what I read about 'Magic Max' in the financial press. I gather he's an arrogant SOB that gets results. In any event, he will resign. Miller will not join Tango's management team."

# # #

Sarah's email is waiting when I return to Paradox from my morning walk.

Carson Fullerton is a 1985 graduate of the Harvard Business School. After graduation, he joined a large New York investment bank and worked as an analyst and investment banker for ten years. He then joined an activist hedge fund that focused on forcing board and management changes at underperforming companies. He failed to make partner at either firm and organized Alpha fifteen years ago with the backing of institutional investors.

He describes himself as a tough negotiator and turnaround specialist. Fullerton had excellent results with Alpha I, his first fund. However, his second fund, Alpha II, was only average. Beta is Alpha III's largest investment. Fullerton's reputation suffered a serious setback when he failed to attract funding for Alpha IV last year.

Fullerton needs to sell Beta to restore his reputation as a smart investor. He purchased Beta in 2017, shortly after Alpha III was organized. Beta's financial results didn't hit the targets he promised the fund's investors, and he replaced Beta's CEO with 'Magic Max' Miller in early 2019.

Miller is a self-promoter and covets his reputation as an aggressive 'super-star' results-oriented CEO. He claims he doesn't like being referred to as 'Magic Max', but always mentions his nickname when he's interviewed. He brags about cutting expenses and several articles describe him as a 'hatchet man'.

#   #   #

A black Rolls Royce is sitting in the no-parking zone in front of Sherman's when I walk up the hill at a quarter to eleven. The driver is the same muscular man in black who greeted me at Fullerton's yacht.

"Good morning, Mr. Wilson. Please wait. I'll place your suitcase in the luggage compartment and open your door. You will find a television and this morning's newspapers in the car. You're welcome to use Mr. Fullerton's internal WiFi system this morning. You will find coffee in a carafe and other beverages in the small refrigerator. The window separating me from your passenger seat is closed, but you can call me on the small handset next to your seat if I can be of assistance."

I grin and say, "Thank you, that's very kind."

8

Palm Beach, Florida

The Rolls stops at the entrance to Portland's private jet terminal and a slender woman in a fitted black jacket opens my door.

"Hi, Steve. I'm Ruth. Carson's jet departs in twenty minutes, so you have time to use the facilities. Walt will take your luggage to the aircraft."

"Thanks. Your arrangements this morning have been exceptionally efficient. I'll just be a few minutes."

"No problem. I'll wait."

Ruth is waiting in the lobby when I return. "This way. We have refreshments and sandwiches on our flight. I've arranged a choice of roast beef, chicken, or vegetarian for you."

"Thank you. Roast beef will be fine."

As we walk out on the tarmac, I see our pilot standing next to the stairs of a six passenger Embraer Phenom 300. Ruth says, "Please go aboard and take the forward-facing seat on the starboard side."

The jet doesn't have enough headroom for my height, so I need to crouch down to swing into my seat. Ruth and the pilot follow me onboard and she places a boxed lunch on each of our small tables. Before she takes her seat, she places a tall glass with a celery stalk on each table. "Our aircraft has a full bar. Welcome aboard, please join me in a Bloody Mary."

"Thank you, but I prefer an ice tea."

Ruth grins and says, "Sure. No problem."

Our pilot announces. "We're cleared for take-off. Please take your seats and fasten your seat belts."

Ruth takes the aft-facing seat across the aisle as I secure my computer case below the table and fasten my seatbelt. When I glance up, Ruth grins as she fastens her seat belt across her short black skirt. She crosses her long legs and extends them into the aisle.

The sound of the jet's engines prevents conversation during take-off and Ruth just smiles in my direction. I open my box lunch once we are airborne. "Nice selection. Thanks for lunch."

"I'll get your ice tea." The jet's headroom is only five feet, so Ruth swings out of her seat and stoops to find tea in the small refrigerator. She pours the tea into a glass of ice and flashes bright green eyes as she leans over to place the tea on my table. "We have a three-hour flight, so we might as well be comfortable. Why don't you take off your blazer?"

"I'm fine, thank you."

Ruth loosens her hair tie, and dark red hair falls to her shoulders. She wiggles out of her black jacket to reveal a sleeveless white top with spaghetti straps.

"That's more comfortable. Now, tell me about yourself. How did you get selected for this assignment?"

"I'm acquainted with Brian Tucker. He asked for my help."

"How frequently does Paradox-Research conduct acquisition due diligence?"

"Brian provided O'Donnell with my firm's profile. Paradox-Research was organized five years ago after I retired from the bank in New York. Paradox provides a variety of services to clients across the country." I ask, "Do you have an agenda for my meetings tomorrow? I'm pressed for time to complete my due diligence. Our meetings must be productive."

"We're having dinner with O'Donnell tonight at The Breakers. He will answer all your due diligence questions. Ready for your Bloody Mary?"

"I'll stay with ice tea. Fullerton doesn't post profiles of his staff. What's your background and how long have you worked for Fullerton?"

Ruth says, "I worked for a national consulting firm and Carson hired me as Alpha's Executive

Vice President a few years ago. The rest is history."

"What can you tell me about Alpha's offer to sell Beta to Tango?"

"Sorry, I'm not authorized to discuss the acquisition. That's O'Donnell's job."

"I understand. If you don't mind, I'll study Beta's financial statements."

Ruth frowns. "Whatever" and picks up her iPad.

9

A black BMW limo is waiting at the Palm Beach private aircraft terminal when we arrive shortly after four.

Ruth says, "Our driver will take us to The Breakers. We have a suite for you and O'Donnell will meet us at the hotel for dinner at seven. That gives you time to check in and we can have a drink before dinner."

I frown. "Beta's offices are located nearby in a suburban office park. I'd like to take a brief tour of their facilities before we go to The Breakers."

"I'll need to call O'Donnell. Excuse me," and she walks into the private terminal.

I'm in the limo reviewing messages on my phone when Ruth opens the door and joins me. "I've arranged for us to tour the facility, but all discussions with Miller will be tomorrow."

A young man greets our limo and says, "Good afternoon, Mr. Wilson. My name is John and I will give you a tour of our facility."

He guides us into a modern three-story dark glass building with a small lobby. Ruth smiles and nods to the men at the security desk. Our guide describes the function of each department as he escorts us through the building. I notice the middle-aged woman at the reception desk directs an icy stare at Ruth as we pass the glass doors leading into the executive suite.

On our way back to the entrance. "I don't recall seeing any accounting or audit functions."

Our guide says, "Alpha's finance department handles all our accounting functions. We manage our global product procurement, assembly contracts, sales, and logistics at this location."

We arrive at The Breakers shortly after six. Ruth walks me to the desk and says, "I need to stop by the office. I've reserved a private room for dinner and O'Donnell will meet you here at seven. I'm forwarding you the updated agenda he emailed me for tomorrow."

A porter directs me to an elevator and describes the hotel as we walk to my suite. "Henry Flagler established The Breakers in 1896 as a luxury oceanside hotel for industry tycoons and elegant socialites. Our hotel has lost none of its historical charm and luxury."

He opens the door and we enter a suite with a balcony featuring an ocean view. A quick tour reveals a spacious living room with a small alcove and desk, a bedroom with a king bed, and a large marble bath. Two doors into the living room are locked, and I assume they link to adjoining rooms if extra space is necessary. I grin when he shows me the suite's fully stocked bar.

I unpack my bag and call Amanda before checking for new messages and emails. "Hi. I'm in Palm Beach and they booked me a suite at The Breakers."

"Nice. How was the jet?"

"Easier than a commercial flight but, so far, the day has been a waste of time. I hope dinner is more productive. How was your day?"

"I'm still exhausted from my trip to Seattle. Hotel rooms all look the same and I'm happy to be back in New York. I prefer the apartment and our neighborhood restaurants are much better than hotel food. I'm getting an early dinner and heading to bed."

My phone flashes *Monet*. "Sarah's calling. Talk to you tomorrow. Love you."

I touch the symbol for my incoming call. "Hi, any updates?"

Sarah says, "First, Ruth's computer has been hacked. The agenda she emailed you had one of those new worms embedded. It's designed to open a back door into your computer system."

"Damn. Did it penetrate my system?"

"No. The firewall we installed detected the virus and blocked entry. She needs better protection."

"I'll send her a text and alert her to the worm on her system. What else?"

"I want to share information on O'Donnell before your dinner tonight. He joined the national accounting firm that audits Alpha's financial statements in 1995 when he graduated from Florida State. O'Donnell was the partner in charge of Alpha's audits when Fullerton hired him as CFO seven years ago."

"What about Max Miller?"

"I'll load Miller's background information on our secure site while you're at dinner."

"Thanks. Please do some research on Ruth Simpson."

"Why? Anything special?"

"Maybe. Everyone stopped talking and looked our direction when we toured Beta's offices."

"That's not unusual when a stranger enters an office."

"True. But they weren't looking at me. Their expressions were throwing daggers at Ruth."

10

I take a quick shower and change my shirt before going to the lobby at six forty-five to meet O'Donnell at seven. I'm admiring the décor in The Breakers historic lobby when Ruth and O'Donnell arrive together at seven-fifteen.

Ruth says, "Steve, this is Patrick O'Donnell, Alpha's chief financial officer."

I smile and extend my hand. "Nice to meet you. Thanks for helping me expedite our due diligence. We're working on a tight schedule."

O'Donnell frowns and ignores my hand. "I'll do what I can."

Ruth signals a member of the hotel staff and she directs us to a private dining room with a round table set for three. Once we're seated, Ruth says, "Thanks for the heads-up about the computer virus. O'Donnell's cybersecurity staff cleaned my laptop. Thankfully, it hadn't spread to our other systems. I must have clicked on an infected link. Sorry it attacked you."

Ruth leans back and grins. "You must have very robust security software."

"Yes. Anything you share with me will be safe."

A server enters with menus. "Would you like cocktails? We're offering a selection of wine with dinner."

O'Donnell says, "Bring me a double vodka on ice with a lime."

Ruth looks at me. I say, "Water is fine."

She gestures to the server. "Bring me the wine selection."

I turn to O'Donnell. "Let's talk about the schedule for tomorrow. The agenda you sent me isn't very specific. I assume you plan to address the questions we emailed to you."

"We've prepared summaries of our monthly management and financial reports for you."

"Summaries might help me focus on specific questions. However, I requested access to detailed sales reports and individual customer transactions. I also need more detail on your intercompany transactions. When is time allotted for me to use the computer terminal I requested?"

"I will answer your questions about our sales and accounting systems tonight. We can review some sample entries tomorrow."

"When will I have access to a terminal?"

Ruth interrupts, "Let's look at our menus and order our dinners before you start your financial discussions."

# # #

Dinner ends abruptly at ten when O'Donnell stands and says, "I have an early meeting tomorrow. It's time for me to head home."

Ruth says, "Thanks. That was helpful."

She turns to me, "May I buy you an after-dinner drink? They have a splendid view from an oceanside bar."

"No, thanks. We didn't accomplish much today. Tomorrow needs to be more productive."

Ruth looks hurt and puzzled. "Sorry, I thought we were making your job easy with the flight today and dinner with O'Donnell. What can I do to make tomorrow meet your expectations?"

I answer. "Just make certain O'Donnell provides me with access to a computer terminal and the detailed information we requested. Tonight's discussion was too general. Dinner was nice, but not very informative."

I hesitate. "Sorry, I don't mean to sound rude. You have been very gracious today and I appreciate your help. Thank you. I'm going up to my suite to prepare for tomorrow. Good night."

"Good night." She grins and blinks her green eyes. "Sleep well."

# # #

I check phone messages on the way to my suite and see text messages from both Brian and *Picasso*.

"Brian, this is Steve. Hope it's not too late."

He laughs. "Investment bankers don't work office hours. How was your day?"

"So far, a waste of time. Do you know why these guys are stonewalling?"

"Stonewalling? I don't understand. Fullerton flies you to Palm Beach on his private jet and arranges a private dinner meeting with his CFO. Looks to me like they're cooperating."

"Appearances can be deceiving. I'm being entertained, not informed. I need to take another call. Talk to you tomorrow."

"Hello, Sarah. I haven't had time to review your information about Miller. Did you learn anything interesting about Ruth?"

"Ruth Simpson received her MBA from Harvard seventeen years ago. She joined Alpha five years ago from a national consulting firm. Her consulting profile listed her as an efficiency expert. She doesn't use social media, but I uncovered posts from terminated employees. Her nickname is 'Ruthless'."

Sarah asks, "What was your impression of O'Donnell?"

"Dresses the part of a Silicon Valley investor. Dark gray slacks, matching collarless shirt, and an expensive sport coat. Kept bouncing his foot and shaking the table at dinner. Arrogant and evasive."

# # #

I'm reviewing Sarah's background report on Miller when I hear the door to the adjoining room open. I turn to see Ruth standing inside my suite's living room. She's wearing the hotel's luxurious bathrobe and holding a bottle.

She laughs. "Don't look so startled." She jingles a hotel key and says, "You must promise not to tell Carson or O'Donnell I booked the adjoining room. I thought a bottle of Champagne might help break the ice."

She pops the cork, walks to the small bar, and tops up two glasses. "Join me" and she makes herself comfortable on the sofa.

"Ruth, I don't know what to say. I make it a rule to avoid personal relationships with clients."

"I'm not a client. I finished one of your books on today's flight and decided it was time to meet the author. Are your stories based on your experiences?"

"Some, but most of the characters are fictional."

Ruth crosses her legs and flutters her bright green eyes as she caresses the seat next to her. "Please sit down. It's rude to keep standing."

I take a seat in the chair across from Ruth. "Why are you here?"

She pouts. "I want to learn more about you."

"Sorry, your visit is making me uncomfortable. Maybe another time."

She stands and gives me a sultry smile and winks. "I'll look forward to another time. See you downstairs at seven for breakfast."

I pick up my laptop, walk to my bedroom, and close the door.

11

I've just stepped out of my shower when *Cassatt* flashes on my phone at six Thursday morning. "Good morning, Sarah."

"Good morning. I have a little more information on O'Donnell. He's married with two daughters in college. He moved from Boston to Florida five years ago and purchased a six-bedroom estate on five acres in West Palm Beach two years ago. The property has a six-car garage, and he recently purchased a Lamborghini. O'Donnell doesn't attend local charitable events, and he doesn't use social media."

"I also have an update on Fullerton and Miller. They have some similar characteristics."

"Such as?"

"They both try to project a tough guy take-charge management style, but avoid face-to-face meetings when executives are fired. Both have blindsided senior executives by announcing changes with a public press release. Terminated executives are called incompetent, lazy, and stupid. Both men demand personal loyalty."

I respond. "Humm ..... I find it difficult to respect executives who don't have the courage to fire any employee face-to-face. I wonder how their tough guy dynamic works inside Alpha if both men require loyalty to themselves. I suspect some executives might feel conflicted. Have any of these former executives taken legal action to protect their reputations?"

"Seldom. Alpha's employment contracts provide for significant termination payments if the executive remains silent."

# # #

Ruth is at the table when I arrive ten minutes early for our seven o'clock breakfast. She says, "I know you're eager to get started today, so I arranged for us to meet O'Donnell thirty minutes early. How did you sleep?"

"Just fine. I've spent most of my career traveling and sleeping in hotels comes easy. Thanks for speeding up today's meeting with O'Donnell."

"Happy to help." She says, "The futures show another positive opening today. Do you invest in the stock market?"

"I manage my retirement accounts, but I'm not an active trader."

"How familiar are you with private equity funds?"

"My firm works with a wide variety of clients." I ask, "What's your management role at Alpha?"

"Nothing specific. I just do special projects for Carson. We have a small staff."

"How many projects have you done at Beta?"

She frowns. "Why do you ask?"

"You were well acquainted with the organization and staff at Beta on our tour yesterday. Our tour guide wasn't necessary."

She grins. "Oh, I visit with all of our investments from time-to-time."

# # #

The BMW limo is waiting under the hotel's portico at eight o'clock. The driver opens our doors and drives us to Alpha's executive offices in West Palm Beach. Ruth leads me to a conference room on the top floor of a high-rise office building with a view of the Intracoastal Waterway. I'm encouraged to see a laptop on the table.

Ruth pours us coffee from a carafe on the credenza and looks impatiently at her watch. She gazes out the window for a few minutes and taps a message on her phone.

O'Donnell joins us a few minutes later. He frowns at Ruth and says, "Sorry I'm late."

I smile and extend my hand. "Good morning. I assume this laptop is for me."

O'Donnell ignores my hand. "Yeah. I've linked this laptop to Beta's reports so we can view them together. I can answer your questions and this should speed up your due diligence work."

He turns to Ruth. "I'd like some coffee."

She smiles, takes a seat at the table across from the open laptop, and gestures to the credenza. "Help yourself."

O'Donnell bristles, but goes to the credenza to pour a cup of coffee. He takes a seat at the table and opens the laptop.

I take the seat to his right and ask, "Where do you want to start?"

O'Donnell is stone-faced. "You requested access to our monthly management reports, so let's look at those."

I pull a yellow tablet out of my laptop case, place it on the table, and say, "That works for me."

O'Donnell says, "Our files are all password protected, but I've provided 'read-only' access on this laptop." He points to the laptop's screen. "That icon links to our reports."

O'Donnell clicks the icon and Beta's laptop opens to an index of management reports.

I say, "Let's start with Miller's year-end report and work our way forward to May. When will June's financial results and management reports be available?"

"We publish financial results within three days, but the July 4th holiday will delay June's reports until after the acquisition is closed and announced."

"Humm …….. I'll need to read Miller's report before I can ask questions."

O'Donnell pushes the laptop my direction. I suppress a grin as I read the self-serving accolades in Miller's report to Fullerton.

My annual results exceeded your aggressive targets and I'm pleased to report each member of my management team earned their maximum bonus.

O'Donnell taps the eraser of his mechanical pencil on the tabletop and gazes out the window while I read. Ruth stands, picks up our coffee cups and refreshes our coffee. She takes the seat next to me and casually looks over my shoulder. I notice O'Donnell's cup is empty as I continue to scroll through Miller's report, making notations on my yellow pad.

When I finish reading, I look over at O'Donnell. "Miller seems more interested in his annual bonus than describing how he achieves Beta's results. I hope his monthly reports include more detail. You must have better information."

"Our executives always focus on good news. That's why my staff reviews every accounting entry and prepares all financial reports. We monitor all financial performance."

"Does Fullerton rely on Miller's reports, or do you prepare separate written reports for him?"

"Alpha has three funds and we own dozens of companies. My staff prepares all monthly financial reports for Fullerton. My comments are always verbal and private."

"Before we move on, I want to review the monthly sales and expense reports for the fourth quarter."

O'Donnell looks at Ruth. "Is that necessary?"

She nods, and he adds an icon to the laptop's screen. "Our sales reports are presented by both product and geography. We expect our growing international coverage to significantly enhance Tango's profitability."

"I understand. That's why it's important to see how Beta's sales teams fit into Tango's operation. Let's open the monthly reports for the fourth quarter."

I take a few minutes to scan the monthly reports and say, "I see over half of Beta's sales occurred in December. Is this a typical pattern?"

O'Donnell smirks. "Miller says his sales teams always work harder at the end of a quarter so they can earn their maximum bonus."

"Have you ever detected bogus sales?"

O'Donnell appears startled. "No. We verify every entry."

I lean back in my chair and say, "Thanks. This is a great start, but I have a lot of reading to do. You're a busy man and I don't want to waste your time while I read. Why don't we reconvene after lunch when I'm ready to ask questions?"

O'Donnell stands. "Good idea," and he gives Ruth a hostile look as he walks out the door.

# # #

At noon, Ruth announces, "We have a lunch reservation at a private club in thirty minutes."

I shake my head. "If it's OK with you, I prefer we have sandwiches delivered and continue working. At this pace, I'm not sure we can finish today. I'll need to spend time with O'Donnell tomorrow morning."

Ruth shrugs. "I'll order sandwiches. Carson asked me to expedite your due diligence. Do you want to meet with O'Donnell this afternoon or tomorrow morning?"

"Let's schedule my meetings with O'Donnell and Miller tomorrow morning."

Ruth grins and says, "That could be interesting," and taps a message on her phone.

O'Donnell opens the door a few minutes later and scowls at Ruth. "Let's step outside."

She smiles. "Sure," and she picks up her cell phone as they walk into the hallway.

I watch their hushed conversation through the conference room's glass partition. O'Donnell looks irritated as Ruth makes a call on her phone. After a few words, she hands her phone to O'Donnell. He shakes his head, scowls my direction, and hands the phone back to Ruth.

She makes another call and returns to our conference room.

Ruth grins. "I've arranged your meetings."

# # #

At six o'clock, O'Donnell opens the conference room door and asks, "How late do you want to work? I have dinner plans tonight."

I lean back in my chair and say, "Humm..... My progress was a little slow." I scan my notes and say, "We can call it a day if I can use the laptop at the hotel tonight."

O'Donnell glares at Ruth and gestures for her to follow him out of the conference room.

Ruth returns in fifteen minutes. "The car's waiting to take us back to The Breakers and we have a reservation for dinner at seven-thirty. We can keep the laptop overnight, but O'Donnell said we need to review the reports together. No copies and I keep the laptop in my possession."

12

When we arrive at The Breakers, Ruth says, "Let's freshen up before our dinner in the dining room. See you in thirty minutes."

I close the door into my bedroom and change into a fresh shirt after my shower. Ruth is waiting in the suite's living room with a glass of wine when I open my bedroom door. She is still wearing her blue blazer but has changed into a less formal pale-yellow top with white pants. She sets her glass on the coffee table and asks, "Ready?"

Ruth reserved a window table at the Seafood Bar for dinner. Once seated, she asks, "You mentioned clients across the country. Do you enjoy travel?"

I shake my head. "Any glamor associated with travel disappeared years ago. Commercial airlines are just a fast bus. But I enjoy working face-to-face with my clients."

She smiles. "I traveled every week during my consulting days. The work and the people were interesting, but I welcomed the opportunity to work with one organization."

I say, "I assume your job includes working with all of Alpha's investments."

"It does, but I don't need to travel every week and Carson welcomes my recommendations. The management teams of the companies we buy are frequently reluctant to make significant organizational changes."

"Is that your role?"

"Carson buys underperforming companies and I evaluate operations and management."

"Did you play a role with Beta's turnaround?"

"Initially. It's easier for an outsider to spot inefficiencies and excess staff. Too many managers measure their importance by the number of employees rather than the efficiency and profitability of their operation."

"Why did Carson recruit Miller as CEO?"

"I recommended some strategic changes at Beta about the time Miller approached Carson at an investment conference. Miller was exploring new opportunities following the sale of his previous company. He convinced Carson he could accelerate Beta's growth and profitability."

"Does Miller support Beta's sale to Tango?"

"Sure. Beta's growth is exceptional and Miller thinks it's a perfect fit with Tango. The proposed structure produces a significant immediate gain for Alpha and our stock ownership provides future value."

"What happens with Miller?"

"He resigns. His employment contract provides for a significant payout when this acquisition is completed and he moves on to his next challenge."

"Alpha will be one of Tango's largest shareholders. Do you see a need for any management changes at Tango following the acquisition of Beta?"

"No, only minor adjustments. We plan to keep Tango's executive team and Miller says he wants to tackle a new project."

# # #

We return to the suite together after dinner and Ruth retrieves Alpha's laptop from her bedroom.

Ruth places the laptop on the small desk and walks to the credenza to pour a glass of wine. "I'll just watch to ensure you don't make any copies. Room service will deliver coffee in about an hour."

Ruth opens her laptop and doesn't say a word for the next two hours while I analyze Beta's monthly reports and examine intercompany transactions. At ten-thirty, I close the laptop, stand, and say, "Thanks. That's it for tonight."

I don't know what to expect when Ruth stands and approaches me. She grins and winks. "See you at seven for breakfast."

I see her wine glass is still half-full when she closes the door to her bedroom behind her.

13

O'Donnell's attitude remains uncooperative, but our Friday morning review of the intercompany relationships goes better than I expect.

Ruth calls the limo for our drive to Beta's headquarters. The receptionist ignores Ruth, but greets me with a stiff smile as she opens the glass security door to the executive suite.

Miller's assistant looks at me. "Mr. Miller is on a conference call and will join you shortly."

Ruth whispers as we sit on a couple of uncomfortable chairs. "Miller expects people to be prompt. He will stand in his office doorway tapping his watch if you're late. If you arrive on time, he keeps you waiting."

At twelve-twenty, Miller emerges from his office in a dark pinstripe suit. "I don't have much time. Follow me."

He opens an adjoining door and leads us into an ornate dining room with a table set for three. He sits at the head of the table with the glare from a floor to ceiling window behind him. It's a bright sunny day and my eyes take a few minutes to adjust.

He looks in my direction. "It's more respectful to wear a suit."

I shrug. "It's hot. I prefer my summer blazer."

"O'Donnell tells me you're doing due diligence for Tango. I'll bet you've never seen a more efficient and profitable company. I've achieved a spectacular turnaround. Tango is fortunate we've agreed to sell Beta to them. I hope I don't have to fix it again."

A male server in a black suit enters the room and places a plate with a chicken-salad sandwich and chips at each of our places. He asks me, "What would you like to drink?"

Miller interrupts. "I only drink water. Sodas are unhealthy and an unnecessary expense. We don't serve alcohol."

I defer to Ruth and suppress a grin when she orders ice tea. I say, "Sounds good, I'll have an ice tea."

Miller says, "O'Donnell says you're impressed with our fantastic sales growth and my superb expense controls. Good thing I had the experience to turn this company around. Fullerton's first management team was a colossal disaster. Expenses were totally out of control and they had no sales strategy. My new people had this place humming within a year."

I ask, "What's your new product strategy to remain competitive? I see you eliminated Beta's research and product development staff."

He laughs. "It's cheaper for me to buy new products rather than waste my money on time consuming research. I've hired a world class sales team. That's why this is such a good fit with Tango."

"I also noticed you eliminated Beta's internal audit and financial staff."

"Damn right. Internal audit was a waste of money. Their questions were an insult to my effective sales strategy. O'Donnell handles our accounting, so I don't need to pay a bunch of green eyeshade bookkeepers."

"What is your sales strategy?"

He smirks. "I hire the best salesmen. Parker is lucky to have the opportunity to buy my fantastic company. I'll need to keep an eye on him and just hope he doesn't screw it up. I've got better things to do than fix this place again."

Miller stands. "I've got work to do."

Ruth grins after he walks out of his dining room and says, "Typical Miller."

# # #

Our driver is waiting and Ruth asks her to swing through a Panera Bread drive-thru on our return to Alpha's office. "Do you want anything? I'm ordering a sandwich."

"Thanks. Lunch was a little skimpy. I noticed Miller's cost cuts didn't include the size of his office and his private dining room."

Ruth says, "Miller views himself as a world-class CEO superstar. He loves it when the press calls him 'Magic Max'. He claims business superstars deserve to be compensated and treated like celebrity sports superstars. That was his driver standing next to the black Bentley parked at the entrance."

"Looks like his driver spends a lot of time in the gym. Does he also serve as security?"

"Sure. Both drivers serve as security. Miller says high profile executives need security. He convinced Carson to hire Walt."

# # #

Ruth and I return to Alpha's conference room for my final meeting with Earl Baxter, the senior partner from the accounting firm responsible for Alpha's annual audits. I expect a private meeting, but O'Donnell introduces Baxter and takes a seat at the table.

I address Baxter. "Thanks for taking time to meet with me today. I don't see any type of audit function at either Alpha or Beta. How do you ensure the accuracy of Beta's financial statements?"

O'Donnell interrupts. "We hire management we trust. Baxter's accounting firm prepares the final certified audit report for our investors."

I keep my gaze on Baxter and say, "I was asking you the question."

Baxter says, "We issue our audit reports in conformity with generally accepted accounting principles and, in our opinion, Alpha maintains an effective system of internal controls."

I frown. "I'm familiar with generally accepted accounting principles. I'm asking about internal controls. How do you ensure the accuracy of Beta's financial statements?"

"O'Donnell's staff prepares financial statements for both Alpha and Beta. We test the amounts and disclosures in conformity with generally accepted accounting principles."

"How much testing do you perform?"

O'Donnell interrupts. "Enough to drive my staff crazy at year-end."

I turn my gaze to O'Donnell. "Weren't you the managing partner for Alpha's account before you joined the firm?"

O'Donnell replies. "Yes, I managed the entire relationship, but Baxter's accounting firm has a deep bench. My deputy took over Beta's audit and Baxter assumed responsibility for the Alpha relationship."

I turn back to Baxter. "What about Alpha's other investments? Who performs those audits?"

"We've assigned other partners to audit Alpha's other operating companies. We issue separate reports on each operating company and a consolidated financial statement for Alpha's year-end reports to the investors in each of Fullerton's private equity funds."

I turn back to O'Donnell. "Tango and Beta use different accounting software. I don't see a provision in the proposed acquisition agreement for transferring Beta's historic financial data to Tango's system. When will you transfer Beta's historic accounting information to Tango?"

He hesitates ...... "Miller and I haven't discussed the transfer of Beta's financial reports."

# # #

Our BMW limo is waiting and our driver heads to The Breakers to pick up our luggage. Ruth says, "I hope your visit has been productive and you plan to complete your report next week."

"I have a few more questions, but the trip has been very informative. I'll discuss my findings with Brian tomorrow."

She smiles. "Anything more I can do before we return to Maine?"

"No. I'll review my notes on the flight and let you know if you can do anything."

"No problem. It will be after ten before we land. I asked the caterers to provide a shrimp dinner on our flight. I hope that's satisfactory."

"Sounds good. It'll be close to midnight before I get back to my boat."

Ruth says, "I have work to do on our return flight and you're welcome to use the aircraft's WiFi connection."

"Thanks, but I won't use the aircraft's WiFi. I'll let you know if I have questions."

The jet is waiting when we arrive at the airport, and it takes off on schedule. We focus on our laptops for an hour until Ruth asks, "Hungry?"

"Yes. Thanks. Dinner sounds good." We both pass on wine and I say, "I was disappointed O'Donnell joined us for my meeting with Baxter."

"I know you requested a private meeting, and I planned to leave. But I thought it was helpful. Didn't you?"

"It was informative. Did you meet John Michaud before his accident?"

"No. I wasn't involved until you replaced Michaud. He flew commercial from Boston for his meetings with O'Donnell, Miller, and Baxter." She pauses, "I understand he was acquainted with Baxter and they had several private meetings."

We both focus on our laptops during the remainder of our flight and Fullerton's Rolls is parked at the terminal when we arrive.

Ruth says, "Walt will drive you back to Boothbay. I'm taking the jet back to Boston."

14

Boothbay Harbor, Maine

My phone buzzes a few minutes after I return to Paradox with my Saturday morning latte and blueberry bar from Dan's Red Cup.

"I hope eight isn't too early after your late-night arrival." Brian continues. "How was your trip?"

"No problem, just picked up a coffee and something to eat. My trip was frustrating. I felt like a dentist. Getting detailed information was like pulling teeth."

"That's disappointing. Were you successful?"

"Mostly. We still have gaps. I need to work on my analysis, but I'm certain Beta's earnings are exaggerated and you'll want to adjust your acquisition price."

"Why? What did you uncover?"

"I have two issues. Miller enhanced Beta's profitability in 2019 with significant cost cuts, including an across-the-board employee reduction, the elimination of the audit and accounting staff, and elimination of new product development."

I continue. "Miller's employment contract provides for Alpha to pay all overhead expenses such as accounting, audit, and legal services. In addition, Miller's executive dining room, his Bentley and driver, and his use of a charter jet are all paid by Alpha. Finally, he created a special bonus pool that's paid by Alpha."

Brian says, "Tango should be able to absorb most overhead expenses and we don't need to worry about Miller's personal expenses. He will not join Tango's management team, so his personal expenses will disappear."

"True. But Tango will absorb some overhead costs and Parker will want to continue a bonus program for the remaining officers and sales staff. Every dollar of expense Miller transfers to Alpha increases Beta's earnings and increases your purchase price by twenty dollars. I'm still tracking the amounts, but Miller has transferred millions of dollars in expenses to Alpha to create the illusion of profitable growth."

"Good point. We can adjust the purchase price to reflect adjusted earnings. What's your second issue?"

"International sales growth is driving the recent increase in profitability. Prior to last year, all sales followed a steady pattern from month-to-month with no growth. In fact, Miller's cost cuts reduced sales in 2019. Last year, all significant international sales growth occurred in the last month of each quarter. I need to verify the accuracy of these last-minute quarterly sales."

Brian asks, "Can you post copies of those monthly sales reports to the secure site?"

"No. O'Donnell didn't give me copies of the reports, but I had sufficient time to make notes. Why doesn't the acquisition agreement provide for Alpha to provide Tango with Beta's historic sales and accounting records?"

"With purchase accounting, we don't need to include or report any of Beta's historical financial information to our shareholders."

"But ……. Doesn't Tango need Beta's historical information to evaluate internal performance?"

"Sure. But O'Donnell said we could take our time transferring the accounting records once we complete the acquisition."

I respond. "He hasn't been willing to share. I suggest you add a requirement for Alpha to transfer Beta's historical accounting records to Tango."

"Good idea. I'll tell our lawyers."

"Remind me. Who suggested Alpha accept Tango's stock as part of this transaction?"

"Fullerton."

"Doesn't Tango have sufficient cash on hand and borrowing capacity to pay all cash for Beta?"

"Yes, but Fullerton wants stock so his fund's investors participate in the future success of Tango's acquisition of Beta."

"OK. Let me get to work. I'll call you tomorrow with an update."

# # #

The harbormaster's boat is arriving at the marina when I return from Red Cup with my mid-morning latte. Jeff says, "Hey, missed you yesterday. What's up?"

"Business travel. Need to complete an assignment before Amanda shows up July 4th. What's the news in Boothbay?"

He replies, "The news is no news from the state medical examiner about our drowning victim."

"I thought it was an accident."

"Probably. I'm told a guy from Boston planned to stay overnight on his sailboat on his way to a business meeting. His wife told the police he was headed to Camden."

"Any kids?"

"His obituary said he had a married daughter in Florida with three grandchildren."

"Damn. His unexpected death must be hard for his family." I frown and say, "I need to get back to work. I'm beginning to regret taking on this assignment."

# # #

The rest of my morning is spent reviewing my notes and analyzing Beta's financial results.

Late morning, I email Sarah and my phone instantly flashes *Picasso*.

Sarah says, "Welcome back. How was your trip?"

"Probably more productive than O'Donnell expected. The internal dynamic at Alpha is weird. Ruth makes a phone call every time O'Donnell resists sharing information. Fullerton wants this deal expedited."

"I'm not surprised." Sarah says, "Rumors are circulating that Fullerton has some unhappy investors. His failure to raise money for a fourth fund was embarrassing. He needs this deal."

"Interesting. It looks like Fullerton hired Miller hoping for a quick turnaround and a fast sale. Miller's reorganization and cost cuts increased earnings but reduced sales two years ago. Beta's recent increase in profitability is due entirely to international sales growth. Miller brags about how his new sales team in London is driving new profit."

Sarah asks, "What do you want me to do?"

"Miller hired this new sales team eighteen months ago. I had sufficient time at the hotel to list the customer accounts assigned to Beta's new office in London. Let's see what you can find out about this new team and their international customers."

# # #

An hour later, the rumble in my stomach lets me know it's past lunchtime, so I walk to Shannon's for a lobster roll. Kim is reading a newspaper when I join her on the dock to eat lunch at her red picnic table.

She asks, "Have you read this article about last week's drowning?"

"No. What does it say?"

"The local police didn't want any publicity, but a Portland reporter read the man's obituary and wrote this story."

Kim hands me the paper.

Man's Body Discovered in Boothbay Harbor

A family visiting on their sailboat discovered a man's body floating in Boothbay Harbor last Friday morning. The family immediately notified the harbormaster. The local police, marine patrol, and the Coast Guard joined the investigation. Calls to marine authorities have not been returned, but my sources suggest the man drowned following an accident.

Louise Michaud said her husband, John, planned to stay aboard his sailboat in Boothbay Harbor Thursday night before a business meeting in Camden on Friday.

The official cause of death has not been announced by the medical examiner, but this accident, once again, highlights the importance of safety measures for all boaters. Water temperatures remain in the mid-fifties and hypothermia can occur within ten minutes and lead to accidental drowning.

Kim says, "You look puzzled."

"I am. Thanks. I need to make a phone call after lunch."

# # #

"Brian, what do you know about John Michaud's accident last week?"

"Nothing. The firm's managing partner called Parker last Saturday. He said Michaud died in a boating accident and we need to find someone fast to complete due diligence. That's all I needed to know, and I called you on Sunday. Why do you ask?"

"Has the firm located his working files?"

"Not yet."

"I'm emailing you a link to a Portland newspaper article. Michaud's boat was on a mooring in Boothbay Harbor. I'd like permission from Michaud's firm or family to board his sailboat if it's still out on the mooring."

"I'll call the managing partner first thing Monday morning."

# # #

Amanda calls Saturday evening at seven and says, "I finished early today and plan to meet two other agents for dinner. It's nice to see people coming back to our neighborhood restaurants. This pandemic has certainly curtailed local business. How's your weekend?"

"Trying to get a handle on my due diligence project. They want my report finished this coming week."

"I plan to leave early on Friday and my flight arrives in Portland at two-thirty. Do you plan to meet me?"

"No. I rented a car in Bangor to drive to Belfast, so your SUV is waiting for you in Portland. I'll grill steaks after you arrive."

"I love this job. But we've been apart for over a month. We need to spend more time together." She laughs. "You better get that report finished!"

"Damn right!" I pause. "I should have known better. This due diligence assignment is more complex than I expected."

"Can you talk about it?"

"I wish I could."

15

I'm heating a cup of yesterday's coffee in the microwave early Sunday morning when I open my laptop and see the email Sarah sent me during the night.

Steve,

Three men organized London's sales office the week after Miller signed their agreement. I traced the sales team to a Chinese distribution firm in Hong Kong. The firm they represented is rumored to be paying bribes to government officials, but no charges have been filed. I uncovered nothing negative about these men prior to the firm in Hong Kong.

I've separated the results of my customer investigation into three groups. First, Beta assigned accounts for a group of existing foreign customers to the new sales team. These customers are all regional subsidiaries of large multi-national firms.

I've organized the new customer accounts the London team has introduced to Beta into groups two and three.

Group two includes new foreign customers with both private and governmental ownership.

Group three includes five new accounts for firms organized a few weeks after the new sales office was opened in London. These new customers were all organized in Malta with the same law firm listed as the registered agent.

Email me when you're ready to talk.

Sarah

I grab a donut in the galley and email Sarah.

A few minutes later, my phone flashes *Renoir.* She says, "Good morning. Sorry, I don't have more solid information to report. The five new accounts in group three are a mystery. The legal structures in Malta disguise their identity."

# # #

I tell Sarah to get some sleep and I reorganize my spreadsheet to show the monthly sales pattern for each of Sarah's three groups of customers. A clear pattern of sales activity emerges when I finish and I email the following results to her.

Sarah,

I've separated your three groups in the attached sales analysis.

Group One > Beta's existing customers assigned to the London sales office show steady monthly activity, but limited growth. These customers pay monthly for Beta's products and services.

Group Two > These new foreign customers represent new sales. However, they have an irregular monthly sales pattern with frequent 'bumps' at quarter-end. Beta's London office is paying an extra commission to third-party agents for sales to these customers. These new customers pay their accounts receivable within ninety days.

Group Three > The results for the five mystery accounts are disturbing. Sales booked for these five firms all occur the last month of each quarter. The accounts are slow to pay, with credits appearing shortly before the 180-day past due date. Let's discuss the attached analysis.

Steve

\# # #

I answer a call from *Matisse* shortly after lunch. Sarah says, "Thanks for giving me time to catch up on some sleep. It was a long night. These sales patterns are suspicious. What more did you uncover?"

"Not enough. I didn't have access to bank account and shipment information for any customers. I need to return to Palm Beach to examine sales, payments, shipping details, and bank account information for London's new customers. Your assignment will be to follow the money and see where it leads."

16

Brian calls mid-morning on Monday. "Thanks for emailing me the link to the news article about Michaud's accident. I hadn't connected the dots with you being on your boat in Boothbay Harbor. I called the firm's managing partner this morning. He said the firm received permission from the police and family to board Michaud's sailboat last Friday. They sent a young associate down to retrieve Michaud's laptop and any files belonging to the firm. The associate said he wasn't able to locate the laptop or its case on the boat and they assume Michaud dropped it when he fell into the water."

"How do they know he fell into the water?"

"The police assume he slipped while trying to board the sailboat."

"Did the police search the sailboat?"

"They sent a forensics team to examine the boat. The team completed their work and released the boat to the family. Michaud's widow is in shock and hasn't moved the boat."

"Did you ask permission for me to search Michaud's sailboat?"

"Yes, the firm welcomes another search. Michaud carried one of those ubiquitous black canvas laptop bags. The boat's name is *Liquidity,* and it's still on its mooring. The combination on the lock is 6789."

"Thanks. I'll go out and take a look."

Brian says, "Whoa. Before you go, how's your report progressing?"

"Finding Michaud's laptop might help. Let's talk later today."

It only takes twenty minutes to lower my dinghy into the water, start the outboard, and locate *Liquidity* on its mooring in the harbor. The aft boarding ladder is still lowered on the transom and it's easy to climb aboard.

An hour later, I sit baffled in the cockpit after my fruitless search of every locker on the sailboat. It's tragic. Michaud appears to have been an experienced and careful sailor. His sailing equipment is neatly organized and his boat is well equipped. The salon, galley, and head are spotless, with the exception of some dried seaweed near the navigation station.

Humm .... Maybe he did slip and fall into the water while trying to board the boat on a dark foggy night. My decks are slippery on foggy mornings.

I return to the marina and tap on the door to Kim's dock office after tying my dinghy to the swim platform on Paradox. "Kim, do you know the name of a diver?"

“Sure. I know several divers who untangle lobster pot lines from props. What’s wrong?”

“I want to search for a lost computer case.”

“At the marina?”

“No. Out in the harbor.”

# # #

Kim alerts me when a Boston Whaler with a dive flag pulls up to the marina after lunch. “Your diver has arrived. Are you ready?”

I explain his mission on our way to the mooring. “We are looking for a black computer case the owner of a sailboat dropped overboard.”

We tie his Boston Whaler’s bow line to a stern cleat on the sailboat and he slips over the side while I occupy my time scanning stock market news and email on my phone.

The diver’s bubbles crisscross the area as he conducts a methodical search of the harbor below the sailboat. He surfaces after an hour.

“Sorry it took so long. You can’t believe the crap people toss overboard.” He hands me a seaweed covered black case. “Is this what you’re looking for?”

Seawater spills from the partially open case as he hands it over the side of his Boston Whaler. The airline tag attached to the handle says John Michaud, and I’m relieved to see the laptop is still inside the case. The papers inside the laptop case are a soggy mess.

"This is it. Well done. Thanks! We can return to the marina." I place the case in the plastic garbage bag I brought along as a temporary evidence bag.

The diver says, "I also found this. Someone dropped a new winch handle." He grins, "Finders keepers."

"Humm ….." I recall seeing an empty winch handle holder in the sailboat's cockpit and say, "Sorry, I think that needs to go with the bag and laptop."

We return to the marina. I pay the diver and wait to call Jeff after the Boston Whaler pulls away from the dock.

"Jeff. I need a favor. Do you have the contact information for the officer in charge of investigating the sailboat accident?"

"Sure. I heard you hired a diver. What did you find?"

"I'll tell you later."

My next call is to Brian. "Good news. The diver I hired recovered Michaud's laptop bag and computer. The papers inside are useless. I suspect the state police want to keep the laptop pending the report from the medical examiner. Michaud's firm will be relieved his laptop's been recovered. The police should return it after they release the medical report."

"Well done. I'll call the managing partner."

I ask, "Did you learn anything about Michaud's meeting in Camden?"

"Michaud's widow told the managing partner her husband scheduled a Friday morning meeting on a yacht in Camden. He planned to stay on his boat Thursday night and his body was discovered Friday morning."

"Does the managing partner know why Michaud wanted to meet with Fullerton?"

"No."

# # #

Monday evening, I email Sarah an update on today's events. Cigar smoke circles my head on my aft deck as I ponder the results of our limited analysis. It's time to tell Brian I need more time to complete my due diligence.

17

A text from Brian greets me Tuesday morning when I step out of my morning shower on Paradox.

Parker wants a status report. We have a conference call at eleven!

I grab a donut, start a fresh pot of coffee, and call Brian.

"I just read your text. I planned to call you this morning. We need to talk before our conference call with Parker."

He asks, "What's up? How soon can you send your report to us?"

"We have a problem."

"Shit! Now what's the problem?"

"I can't verify the accuracy of their new foreign sales with the limited information O'Donnell has provided. I need a private conversation with Baxter."

Brian sighs. "Wasn't a private meeting on your schedule in Palm Beach?"

"It wasn't private. Both O'Donnell and Ruth stayed for my meeting with Baxter. He seemed nervous and his responses sounded like policy statements from an accountant's handbook." I pause and ask, "Did Michaud say anything to you about his meetings with Baxter?"

"No. Michaud didn't discuss any of his meetings with me. I hope you connect with Baxter before our call with Parker. I get paid when this deal gets done."

# # #

I expect a receptionist and am surprised when Baxter answers his phone at eight-thirty. "Good morning, you start early. This is Steve Wilson and I have a few more questions."

Baxter replies after a pause. "I have a busy morning. What do you need?"

"Thanks. I don't have questions concerning Beta's audited financial statements. I'm curious what you and John Michaud discussed in your private meetings."

Baxter pauses and slowly responds. "John was an old professional friend. He was a few years older and my mentor for my entire career. I was heartbroken when I learned about his accident."

"I'm sorry. I never met John. Everyone describes him as a true professional with the highest integrity."

Baxter says, "Yes. That certainly describes John. Most people are surprised to learn he showed an amazing sense of humor with friends and family."

"I believe he was questioning Beta's recent sales growth. Is this what you discussed in your private meetings?"

A long pause .... "Our conversations were personal."

I call Brian after we disconnect.

"My call with Baxter was unproductive. I'm ready to explain my problem at eleven."

"Damn! Hold on, I'll try to connect Parker now."

I'm on hold for five minutes before I'm connected to our conference call.

"Steve, this is Vince Parker. What the hell is going on? Brian tells me you won't issue your report this week."

"I can't verify Beta's sales growth and, as a result, I can't verify their earnings."

"Why? Can't we rely on Beta's audit?"

"I just got off the phone with Earl Baxter, Beta's independent audit partner, and he won't discuss his meeting with Michaud or Beta's audit."

"You didn't answer my question. Why can't we rely on Baxter's audit?"

"We've uncovered some very suspicious transactions related to Beta's new sales team in

London. I need to verify the accuracy of Beta's sales to a group of new foreign customers."

Parker is slow to respond. "How important are these sales?"

"These new foreign customers represent nearly all of Beta's sales growth."

Brian interrupts. "How much time do you need?"

"At least another week."

"What do I tell O'Donnell?"

"Just tell him I need another week."

Brian sighs. "OK. But we need to be ready for some nasty feedback!"

Parker says, "That's OK. I won't do this deal until we can trust the numbers."

# # #

Kim and Jeff are talking at the picnic table when I return from Shannon's with a fish sandwich for lunch. Jeff says, "OK. What's up? Why are you so interested in the dead guy's sailboat?"

"It might be related to a project I'm evaluating."

Kim asks, "Evaluating or investigating? The diver said he recovered a laptop."

I shake my head. "You guys are tough. I'm working on a project for a client. The owner of the sailboat was working on the same project and his firm asked me to look for his laptop. I was just doing a favor for a client."

Jeff laughs. "Likely story."

18

Brian calls Wednesday morning. "I called O'Donnell yesterday after our call with Parker. His assistant said he wasn't available. He didn't return my call until this morning. O'Donnell was seriously pissed and hung up on me when I told him you need another week."

"What's next?"

"Damned if I know. Oops, O'Donnell's calling. I'll get back to you."

Brian calls ten minutes later. "O'Donnell is really pissed. He said he's been cooperating with your requests and Miller says additional time is not necessary."

"And?"

"I said Parker won't proceed with negotiations until he receives your due diligence report."

"What did O'Donnell say?"

"Nothing. He hung up on me."

I say, "Interesting, Miller's not calling the shots. Rumors suggest some of Fullerton's investors are getting restless and he needs a deal to enhance the performance of his fund. Tango is the natural buyer. That's why Fullerton approached Parker."

Brian says, "I need to keep this deal on track. How do we contact Fullerton?"

"I don't think that's necessary. If Fullerton wants this deal to move forward, then he'll contact you. I'll start planning my next step."

Brian asks, "If O'Donnell calls, what do I tell him you need?"

"I need more than reports. O'Donnell needs to provide me with access to individual customer transactions for sales, accounts receivable, and shipping information. I need to examine Beta's accounting and bank transactions to verify what products certain customers purchased, where they were shipped, and who paid. That's the only way for me to verify these sales. I'll need to go back to Palm Beach."

Brian sighs. "Don't hold your breath."

I say, "One more thing. I believe Michaud had similar concerns. We need to expedite recovery of any data on his laptop. Please ask the accounting firm to contact the state police."

# # #

I'm walking to Red Cup for a late-morning latte when my phone flashes *Ruth Simpson*.

"Good morning, Ruth."

"Good morning to you, Steve. I understand you need more time to finish your report. Carson is disappointed we can't announce the transaction as scheduled. What can I do to help?"

"Our trip to Palm Beach was helpful, but I still need more information to complete my report. We need to arrange another trip to Palm Beach to verify the data in my analysis. O'Donnell needs to give me access to Beta's customer accounts to complete my report."

"Is this trip necessary?"

"I could do the analysis remotely if O'Donnell gives me access to Beta's accounting system. I can't issue my report without this additional information, and Tango won't proceed without my due diligence report."

"Understood. I'll talk to Carson."

# # #

Thirty minutes later, I receive a call from Ruth.

"Carson is not happy, but he had me call O'Donnell. Carson wants him to cooperate and give you what you need so we can complete the sale of Beta to Tango. When do you want to go to Palm Beach? I can arrange a jet as early as tomorrow."

"That's fine. What time?"

"Walt will pick you up at nine o'clock."

"OK. Please make certain I will have access to Beta's customer accounts or we're wasting everyone's time."

# # #

I'm dreading my next conversation with Amanda; she expects me to be in Boothbay when she arrives Friday night. So, I text her.

Call me when you have time.

She replies thirty minutes later.

We need to talk. I'll call later tonight.

# # #

I'm at my laptop, reviewing Sarah's research, when Amanda calls me at eight.

I bite the bullet. "Hi, thanks for calling. I'm really sorry, but I need to go back to Palm Beach tomorrow. I hope to be back Friday night so we can enjoy July 4th weekend together."

Amanda sighs. "I'm not coming."

"What? Why?"

"Mark had a staff call late today. Have you been following Delta?"

"Not closely. We're both vaccinated. Delta only seems to be a threat to unvaccinated people. Why?"

"One of my vaccinated team members tested positive for Covid after I returned to New York. I'm in quarantine until I get the results from my Covid test tomorrow morning. Mark is concerned about breakthrough cases and doesn't want us to take any unnecessary risks. He wants vaccinated staff to limit travel and work remotely again. I could work from our New York apartment but plan to organize my assignments and return to Portland."

I ask, "Mark really expects Delta to become a serious outbreak?"

"Our internal medical projections are ominous, and he wants to get ahead of any outbreak. Working remotely and using video systems has worked well for over a year, so it's no problem to continue."

"Damn. I hope your test is negative. When do you get your results?"

"I get the first results tomorrow. I'll text you."

"Thanks ...... Working from Portland will make it easier for your weekend visits to the boat and I can spend some time with you in Portland. Weird, this might be good news for us."

She says, "I still have unused vacation time, so we can plan more cruises this summer. I'll get moved this weekend if I'm still negative after a second test on Friday. Hopefully, I can come later this weekend."

19

Palm Beach, Florida

I'm pacing the sidewalk in front of Sherman's bookstore Thursday morning when Walt pulls up thirty minutes late. No greeting today. He frowns as he pops the trunk and doesn't help me with my suitcase. He slams my door as I place my laptop case on the seat next to me. I'm aware of a solid 'click' as he locks my doors from the driver's seat.

No coffee or newspapers today.

# # #

Ruth welcomes me with a smile when I exit the Rolls. I hear her ask Walt, "Why are you late?"

Walt remains seated and says "traffic". He pops the trunk from the driver's seat and, after an awkward pause, Ruth retrieves my suitcase.

I take the handle. "Thank you, but I can take my bag."

Ruth rolls her suitcase through the private air terminal and onto the tarmac. We walk to the same type of jet as our last flight, but it's a different aircraft and crew. I ask, "Does Fullerton always charter with NetJets?"

Ruth smiles. "Very perceptive. You don't miss much."

"I don't plan to miss anything important."

She grins and tilts her head. "I don't expect you will."

Embraer Phenom 300 @ NetJets

"What are my arrangements in Palm Beach?"

"Similar to your last visit. O'Donnell is not loading reports on the data site. He will provide a laptop with 'read only' access to the information you requested. Is that satisfactory?"

"It should be."

This jet has all forward-facing seats, and Ruth sits across the aisle from me. Once airborne, she drops to her knees and places a cup of coffee and small pastry from the compact galley on both our small tables. She says, "Make yourself comfortable. Just let me know when you're ready for a box lunch."

"We won't arrive at the office until two. How late can we work tonight?"

"As late as you wish. Beta's laptop will have access from the hotel."

She pauses, smiles, and flashes her bright green eyes. "I've booked the same suite."

She again removes her jacket, revealing a sleeveless white top with spaghetti straps, and stretches her long legs into the aisle. She is absorbed reading her iPad for the rest of our flight.

# # #

We take the BMW limo to Alpha's downtown office and enter the small conference room we used previously with a view of the Intracoastal.

I ask, "How soon will O'Donnell join us?"

"I told his assistant we arrived and expect coffee to be delivered."

Five minutes later, O'Donnell opens the door but remains standing with his arms crossed after placing a laptop on the table. "What do you need from me?"

I gesture to Beta's laptop. "I'm not familiar with your accounting system and would appreciate a tutorial. Please show me how to access and review the customer transactions used to create your income and expense reports."

"Why? Don't you trust my reports?"

"Your reports are fine, but they only summarize the underlying transactions. I need to test some transactions to better understand the business Tango will buy from Alpha. I'm certain you reviewed the same details before you purchased Beta."

I remove my blue blazer, place it on the back of the chair, and sit next to Beta's laptop. "I'm ready to start."

He frowns but sits at the table. "What do you want to know?"

I remove a yellow pad from my laptop case and place it on the table. "Just walk me through the steps required for me to access and view the detailed customer information."

O'Donnell opens Beta's laptop and guides me through the tedious steps required to view Beta's customer information. Ruth has a puzzled expression as I ask basic accounting questions and take detailed notes.

Thirty minutes later, I say, "Thanks. I think I can follow the required steps with my notes. You've been very helpful. We'll call you if I need more help."

O'Donnell stands. "I've got a busy day. Don't expect a quick response."

20

Thursday afternoon, Ruth is working on her laptop while I review customer accounts and start filling my yellow pad with detailed notes.

At five, I hear O'Donnell tap on the conference room's glass panel and he gestures to Ruth to join him. She nods, steps into the hallway, and closes the door. O'Donnell's voice is loud enough to overhear part of their conversation, but I can't discern Ruth's quiet responses.

O'Donnell gestures at me. "What's he doing? Has he said anything?"

O'Donnell continues. "He asked me a lot of stupid questions. He can't be too bright. Let's get him outta here by six."

When Ruth returns. "O'Donnell wants to close up the office at six. Let's plan to head to the hotel in an hour. I'll make a reservation for dinner."

# # #

Ruth picks up two keys from reception, a porter takes our bags, we ride the elevator together, and he opens the door to the suite. She tips the porter and winks. "I'll freshen up in my room.

Our reservation at The Ocean Grill is at seven. We can work as late as you like after dinner."

"Thanks. A dinner break sounds good." A hot shower and clean shirt brighten my outlook after a tedious afternoon. Ruth is waiting in the suite's living room with a glass of wine when I open my door.

She sets her glass on the coffee table and says, "Time to go."

Once we're seated, she asks, "You didn't ask questions this afternoon. Do you have access to the information you want? You sure take a lot of notes."

"Yes. It's a tedious step-by-step process and my outline helps me stay on track. A few more hours tonight and I should be prepared to ask Miller a few questions at our meeting tomorrow morning."

She raises an eyebrow. "That should be interesting."

"I noticed Miller didn't acknowledge you at our lunch on my last visit."

"He has difficulty relating to people who don't work for him."

"I understand he demands personal loyalty from his staff."

"You are doing your homework." She pauses. "I assume you figured out how to use our accounting systems."

"Yes. O'Donnell's guidance was helpful."

Ruth smiles. "I don't think you needed any guidance."

I look down at the menu and say, "Let's order, so I can get back to work."

# # #

We return to the suite, and I'm relieved when Ruth moves to the sofa with her laptop and a glass of wine. At eleven o'clock, I close Beta's laptop and say, "That does it for tonight. I'll have a few questions for O'Donnell at eight-thirty and Miller at ten tomorrow morning. With any luck, we should be ready to depart around noon."

I'm still seated when Ruth walks over to the small desk, places her hand on my shoulder, and picks up Beta's laptop with her free hand. Her green eyes gaze down at mine. She raises an eyebrow. "See you at seven for breakfast?"

I stand and say, "Yes, thank you, you've been very helpful."

She closes the door to her bedroom and I notice her wine glass is still half full.

21

I hear room service arrive at six-thirty Friday morning. Ruth is sitting on the sofa with a cup of coffee when I open my door.

She smiles and says, "I've ordered breakfast to be delivered at seven. There's coffee for you on the counter. I thought you might want privacy if you want to work or have questions."

"Thanks, but I'm ready for our morning meetings."

She grins. "Why are you so interested in the sales and accounts receivable for Beta's new foreign customers?"

"They account for all of Beta's sales growth and the increase in reported earnings. I just want to verify the results." I pause. "I was curious if it was you or O'Donnell tracking the accounts I've been reviewing."

She grins. "You don't miss much. It was me. I don't know about O'Donnell."

I say, "Breakfast has arrived."

# # #

Ruth is pacing when O'Donnell finally joins us in the small conference room at nine-fifteen.

I note her sarcastic tone when she says, "Nice of you to join us. You're forty-five minutes late and we have a tight schedule this morning."

"I'm a busy man." He turns to me. "What do you want?"

I take a seat at the conference table. "I just have a few questions. This shouldn't take long."

He remains standing. "OK. Get on with it."

"How do you verify the creditworthiness of your new foreign customers?"

"These are long-term customers of our new sales team in London and they have a long history of satisfactory payment."

"How did you verify their prior payment history?"

"The new sales team assured me they had a solid payment history."

"How do you explain the increase in accounts receivable from London's new customers?"

"It's not unusual. All new customers delay payment to test our policy of adding late charges for payment after sixty days."

"Humm .... I see no record of you charging late payment fees. Do you always waive fees for new customers?"

"Miller asked me to waive late payment charges and we don't consider a foreign account past due until it hits 180 days. Payments from foreign customers take longer to process." He looks at Ruth. "Your meeting with Miller is at ten. You don't want to be late."

O'Donnell turns toward the door and I say, "I have a few more questions." He pauses and I say, "If I understand your system, you pay your sales teams their commissions and bonuses when an order is received, not when the customer pays. Is that correct?"

He steps to the doorway. "Sure. Sales is not responsible for collecting payment."

I ask, "Is that another Miller policy?"

O'Donnell glares at me. "You don't want to be late," and he walks out of the conference room.

# # #

Miller is standing in his office door tapping his watch when we arrive at ten minutes after ten. He scowls. "You're late, I'm busy, and you're wasting my time."

I smile. "Then let's get started. Your office or the conference room?"

He turns, walks into his office, and sits behind his extra-large desk in front of a large window. Ruth guides me into the office, gestures for me to sit on the sofa, and sits on a side chair next to the sofa. My seat on the sofa avoids being blinded by the bright sunlight from the window behind Miller's desk.

Miller is glaring at Ruth when I say, "I have a few questions about international sales."

He interrupts, "Listen. My amazing London sales team transferred their international accounts to us. I recruited a fantastic group and your questions are insulting."

"How often do you expect to get paid? Do you expect Tango to accept their slow pay accounts?"

"Of course, that's in the agreement."

"Then, if you were me, wouldn't you want to verify the creditworthiness of these new customers?"

"You can take my word they are creditworthy."

"Humm ……. You know that's not acceptable."

Miller stands red faced. "Screw both of you. Get out of my office."

I remain seated. "I have more questions."

Miller just glares at Ruth and storms out of his office.

Ruth smiles. "That's a first."

# # #

Ruth signals the limo and asks, "Anything more you need, or is it time to head to the airport?"

"I'm finished. We can head to the airport."

"Anything you want me to tell Carson?"

"Not yet." I ask, "Why are you being cooperative and those guys are so belligerent and evasive?"

"Nothing new. Male executives resent female consultants interfering in their domains. It's simple, they don't like the fact that Carson asked me to expedite their transaction."

"Why does Carson want a large stock position in Tango after the acquisition?"

"Miller says, with proper management, earnings should explode after the acquisition and Alpha should benefit by the increase in value."

# # #

Ruth arranges for the jet to depart early. We arrive in Portland late-afternoon, and Walt is waiting with the Rolls.

Ruth says, "I'm joining you for the drive to Boothbay and going on to Camden today."

22

Boothbay Harbor, Maine

It's just six o'clock when I walk down the dock to Paradox. I toss my suitcase on the settee, open my laptop on the desk, and call Brian. He asks, "How was your trip? Did you get what you need?"

"I think so. Alpha has a very interesting internal dynamic. Both O'Donnell and Miller are evasive, and Ruth is being incredibly helpful. She confirmed Fullerton wants her to expedite this transaction."

I continue. "Alpha will only have a ten percent ownership, but Fullerton's proposed agreement adds three new board members to Tango's new ten-person board. That's three times Alpha's stock ownership. Has Parker agreed to let Fullerton add three new board members?"

"No. That's just Fullerton's proposal. O'Donnell says Beta will represent over twenty-five percent of combined sales, so Fullerton should have three seats on the board. O'Donnell's proposed agreement names O'Donnell, Ruth, and one unnamed person as the new board members."

I ask, "Aren't you concerned about the amount of control Fullerton would have?"

"That's just their proposal. We're not discussing board seats until we agree on a price. There's no deal if we can't agree on the price."

I say, "I'd be careful. Miller said he hopes Parker doesn't screw up the combined company, so he has to fix it again. Fullerton has a history of promising no management changes before he buys a company, but he always makes changes after a deal is closed."

"Fullerton's not buying Tango. We're buying Beta."

"You're paying in stock and Fullerton will have three board seats. Ruth seems to view this transaction as another management team for her to monitor."

"Humm ...... I see your point."

"I suggest you limit Fullerton to one board seat equal to his stock ownership. I suspect Miller expects to be the third board member."

Brian says, "I'll discuss it with Parker."

I continue. "I'll work on my sales analysis over the weekend. Let's schedule a call with Parker early next week."

# # #

As planned, Sarah calls Friday evening and asks, "How did it go?"

"Better than I expected. O'Donnell didn't block access and Beta's laptop had read-only access to all customer accounts."

"Did you get the information we need?"

"More than I expected. I located the names and bank account numbers for Beta's customers and the third-party agents receiving commissions for sales to the accounts in group two. Beta pays sales staff a commission on each sale and they earn a bonus if they hit their sales target at quarter-end. Beta's London office pays agent commissions to middlemen, not sales staff."

Sarah asks, "What about the bank accounts for the customers in group three?"

I laugh. "There aren't any."

"What? You didn't find any bank accounts."

"That's right. None of the sales and accounts receivable transactions for the customers in group three are cash transactions. No cash changes hands. It looks like a Ponzi scheme using products rather than cash."

Sarah sighs. "I'll be damned. That's a first."

"The only cash transactions are the agent commissions paid on group three accounts."

"How can I help?"

"Let's divide and conquer. I'll email you the bank account numbers for agent commissions paid in groups two and three. You track the money and I'll document shipping records and accounts receivable information for our five mystery customers in group three."

"Sounds good."

I say, "One more thing. Ruth has been tracking my activity."

"Did you disguise your interest?"

"I started opening random files to help disguise any obvious pattern when the screen sharing symbol appeared on Beta's laptop. I didn't disguise my questions about foreign customers with O'Donnell and Miller, but I didn't ask about any specific accounts."

# # #

I'm focused on my shipping analysis when my phone flashes *Amanda*. "What's the news?"

"Good news. My test today was negative, and I reserved a car in New York to drive to Portland Saturday morning. How's your project?"

"It's not finished, but I would love a visitor."

"I'll call you tomorrow after I get settled."

# # #

I want to finish my analysis before Amanda arrives and document product shipments until two Saturday morning. When I finish, I send Sarah an email to call me in the morning.

23

I struggle out of my bunk at six-thirty Saturday morning and place a cup of yesterday's coffee in the microwave. I check for Sarah's email after splashing water on my face.

You were up late. I'll call at eight.

Whew. That gives me time for a walk and a fresh latte from Red Cup. I pour the day-old in the galley sink and start my day.

I'm just finishing a bowl of fruit when *Chagall* flashes on my phone.

"Hi, Sarah. Thanks for giving me time."

"No problem. Were you able to track the shipments?"

"The products sold to these five mystery firms are shipped from China to Beta's European distribution center in Rotterdam. The sales records show each of our mystery customers has their purchases shipped fifteen miles down A15 from Rotterdam to the same small warehouse in Dordrecht. Each device is about the size of a hardcover book, so these customers don't require a large storage facility."

"Beta's accounting records show these five mystery customers all purchase the same control device on credit with payment due within 180 days. They return the control devices to Beta after 160 days for a credit to their account. A few days later, they order new devices to offset the credit. At the end of the quarter, they place a new order to hit Beta's quarterly sales goal."

Sarah says, "What a spiderweb. When the dust clears, they increase sales and avoid accounts receivable older than 180 days."

I continue. "It's a complex Ponzi scheme replacing old sales with more new sales. The outstanding customer receivables increase with each transaction, but the books never show a past due account. No cash changes hands. It's all just bookkeeping entries for transfers of equipment to and from the Dordrecht warehouse."

Sarah sighs, "That explains why you didn't find any bank account information for the customers in group three."

She continues. "The agent commissions paid for sales in group two went to different accounts at different banks. The payments were all made to shell companies with law firms as registered agents. I don't know who received the money but these commissions are linked to sales in countries notorious for political kickbacks."

I ask, "What about the five mystery accounts in group three?"

"Different story. All these commissions are paid to bank accounts in Switzerland owned by the same shell company organized in Malta."

I respond, "Humm ……. These guys hit their quarterly sales targets with last-minute sales to group three's fake accounts. I'll bet folding money they pay the agent commissions on these fake sales to themselves."

Sarah asks, "What's next?"

"I need to decide how to explain our findings to Brian and Parker."

"Why not just show them our exhibits?"

"We have a series of suspicious transactions based on my notes. We don't have documents to prove Beta is paying illegal kickbacks and committing fraud. This is a due diligence assignment, not an FBI investigation."

# # #

"Brian, we need to set up a call with Parker. It's time to discuss my findings."

"Can it wait until Tuesday? I hate to track him down on the 4th of July weekend."

"I think he will want to hear my update."

"Can you brief me in advance?"

"I prefer to discuss it with both of you at the same time. I'm not sure what our next step should be."

"This sounds serious."

"It is. Please, see if you can set up a call with Parker."

# # #

I'm expecting a call from Brian and exhale a sigh of relief when I see *Amanda* flash on my phone Saturday afternoon.

I answer. "Hi. It's great to hear your voice. When will you arrive?"

"I'm ready to drive down today if you have time for a visitor."

"Damn right I want to have a visitor! How soon can you be here?"

"Couple of hours. How's your project? I don't want to interfere."

"I think my project is done."

# # #

I grab my bike and ride to Hannaford's. It's a quick stop to select two filets, fresh asparagus, and a bottle of Pinot Noir to put in my backpack for tonight's dinner.

I race back to place my purchases in the boat's refrigerator and I'm resting at a picnic table next to the city's waterfront parking lot when Amanda's SUV comes down the hill. She's filling out the honor system card at the ticket stand when I sneak up behind her. "Hey lady, have time for a kiss?"

She turns, flips her blond ponytail to one side, and gives me a long kiss before I can utter another word. We both jump when the car behind her SUV gives a short beep on the horn and we see two teenage girls giggling and gesturing to move.

Amanda flashes a smile, hops back in her SUV, and finds a parking space. I follow, open her door, and greet her with a long hug and kiss. She grabs her backpack from the front seat and I ask, "Anything in the boot?"

"No. It's easy to travel between New York, Portland, and Paradox. I just needed to organize my work projects before departing New York. No need to pack and unpack when anything I need is already in each location."

We walk hand-in-hand across the parking lot, up the hill, and down the street toward Kim's marina. "I'm glad you made it."

We've just started down the dock to Paradox when Kim shouts, "Hey, Amanda!" and rushes to meet her.

They give each other a hug and Kim says, "Glad you're here. Maybe you can get this hermit to be more sociable. He's been working too much."

Amanda winks at Kim. "After I get some private time."

Kim laughs and winks in return and says, "Later."

24

Sunday, July 4th

Brian calls Sunday morning. I say, "Give me a minute" and signal Amanda. She waves as she goes for a walk.

"Go ahead."

Brian says, "I left a message for Parker yesterday afternoon and he returned my call a few minutes ago. I have him on hold. Are you ready to talk?"

The next voice says, "This is Vince Parker. Brian says we have a problem."

I answer. "That's correct. I can't verify the sales growth reported by Beta's new marketing team in London."

Brian exclaims. "Shit. How much more time do you need?"

"It's not a question of time. I believe some of those sales don't exist."

Parker says, "Did I hear you right? They don't exist?"

"That's correct. I can't verify some of Beta's sales."

Brian asks, "How many? How will this impact our price?"

"If you proceed, then I recommend you disallow all sales to all new customer accounts at the London sales office."

Brian stammers. "Damn. You can't be serious."

Parker asks, "How do we explain this to Fullerton?"

I respond. "We don't. Beta has a series of transactions I can't verify, but I have no documents to prove anything illegal. You don't want to open a door to legal retaliation."

Brian says, "Are you sure you can't verify these sales with more time?"

"I'm sure."

Brian continues, "What if we just discount the price and work with London to correct any problems?"

"I believe you risk becoming a party to illegal foreign payments and accounting fraud."

Parker interrupts. "That's enough reason. I don't want any legal risk with this transaction."

Brian asks, "What do I tell O'Donnell?"

Parker says, "That's easy. Tell him we have no further interest in acquiring Beta. We don't need to tell him why."

"When do I call O'Donnell?"

Parker laughs. "No time like the present. Let's get this over with so I can get back to work on Tuesday."

#   #   #

I disconnect, and Brian calls before I can place my phone back on my desk. He asks, "You're sure there is no way to verify those sales and we can get this back on track? I can always ask for more time."

"You don't want to take your client down that road. Sorry, you owe it to Parker to kill this deal. You don't want Tango to buy this Pandora's Box. I believe it holds some nasty surprises."

A long pause ………………."OK. I'll call O'Donnell."

#   #   #

Amanda returns and says, "Hope your call was successful."

"I should know later today. I'm ready for a walk and a Red Cup latte."

Dan greets Amanda with a broad smile when it's our turn to order, "Hey, great to see you. It's nice to see a smile on Steve's face for a change."

Brian calls while we are sipping our coffee at the Public Landing. I nod at Amanda. "Give me a minute" and walk to an open area.

Brian says, "I just told Parker that I talked with O'Donnell and the deal is dead."

"What was O'Donnell's reaction?"

"He was pissed I called him on a Sunday morning during a three-day holiday weekend. He kept insisting I give him a reason when I told him the deal is off." Brian hesitates …….. "So, I told him you couldn't verify the sales growth in London."

"Damn. What did he say?"

"I heard him swear, and the line went dead."

"Shit! Brian, I think you just opened Pandora's Box."

25

I'm in a daze when I return to our picnic table. Amanda says, "You look terrible. What's wrong?"

"I wish I could tell you."

"You still want to dinghy over to the Lobster Pound for lunch?"

"No. I've lost my appetite. Let's take a walk."

Amanda stops at a local gallery to admire the new painting in the window. We're holding hands and she feels my fingers tense up when my phone buzzes. I tense up again when I hear the ding for a message.

She turns with a quizzical look and asks, "You expecting a call?"

"Not sure." I squeeze her hand before reaching into my jeans pocket for my phone and listen to the message.

I smile, return the phone to my pocket, and say, "That might be the first time I welcome a robocall offering my last chance to renew my non-existent car's warranty."

Amanda frowns. "What's wrong?"

"I expect some nasty feedback concerning my due diligence assignment."

# # #

We're sharing a glass of wine on the aft deck Sunday evening when Amanda says, "Kim's right, we're both too preoccupied with work. Was your client unhappy with your report?"

"It wasn't the answer they expected to hear."

"Why did they hire you?"

"The man doing the assignment died in a boating accident and his firm didn't have an experienced replacement."

"Oh. That explains the short time. I expect his report gave you a head start."

"No, it didn't. We can't locate his notes or a copy of his report. His laptop went overboard during his accident."

"His firm didn't have a backup system?"

I reply, "He was retired and using his personal laptop."

"What about his personal backup?"

"The firm's managing partner told the investment banker his widow didn't know the password he used to protect his due diligence files."

26

Amanda has a spring in her step Monday morning as we navigate a path to Red Cup through the throng of tourists waiting to board the tour boats.

The picnic tables at the Public Landing are occupied, so we lean against the railing overlooking the harbor to admire a passing sailboat. Amanda says, "You look worried. That's out of character. Can you talk about it?"

"Not yet. I feel conflicted about my next step."

"Why do you need a next step if your project is completed?"

"Too many unanswered questions." I pause and point to a line of tourists boarding the harbor tour boat. "They have the right idea. Let's take the dinghy out for a private tour of the harbor. How about a stop at the Burnt Island lighthouse?"

She responds with a soft kiss. "Wonderful idea."

My dinghy is tied to the swim platform, so I toss in the life vest bag, grab my handheld VHF, and climb aboard to start the outboard. Amanda joins me and as we push away, she says, "Hey, you have a leak. There's water sloshing around."

I laugh and say, "Sloppy seamanship. I've done a

couple of evening tours to clear my head, but forgot it rained overnight a couple of days ago."

She says, "You are too preoccupied."

As we pass an empty mooring ball, I say, "Looks like they finally moved the boat."

Amanda asks, "What boat?"

"Oh. That's the mooring where my predecessor had the accident on his sailboat."

"The guy's accident was here? What happened?"

"Jeff said they think he slipped and fell in the water. Still waiting on the medical examiner to confirm if drowning or hypothermia was the cause of death."

"They've had time to complete the autopsy. You should know the answer this week."

# # #

We return from our visit to Burnt Island and a tour of the harbor in time for a hot shower on Paradox before dinner.

I'm tense every time my phone buzzes and freeze when I see *Ruth Simpson* flash on my phone. I gaze at the screen, waiting to hear the message ding. My finger twitches as I touch the icon.

Steve, this is Ruth. O'Donnell called Carson this afternoon and said Brian Tucker just called him to say the deal is off. O'Donnell said Tucker didn't provide a reason.

Please call me. Thanks.

Amanda looks up from the galley and says, "That's a strange look. What's up?"

"I just listened to a very strange message."

"Was it the call you've been dreading?"

"Yes."

"Do you need to return it? Do you want privacy?"

"Not tonight. I'll return the call tomorrow after you head back to Portland. Let's enjoy your shrimp dinner."

27

I wait until nine Tuesday morning to call Brian. "Has anyone at Alpha or Beta contacted you or Parker?"

"No. Parker just called and asked me the same question. All quiet."

"Not quiet enough. Ruth left me a strange message last night. She said O'Donnell didn't tell Fullerton about your Sunday morning call until Monday afternoon. She also said you didn't give O'Donnell a reason."

Brian says, "That's not true. I heard him swear after I told him you couldn't verify London sales." He pauses. "Sorry I screwed up, but he knows the reason."

"Humm .... Why didn't he tell Fullerton?"

Brian says, "Damned if I know. Afraid of his reaction?"

"Maybe. Should I call Ruth? It might head off a call from Fullerton to Parker."

"The deal's dead. Our attorneys say we have no obligation to talk."

# # #

Ruth calls and leaves similar messages every couple of hours during the day. I'm enjoying a glass of wine late afternoon at Kim's picnic table with friends from another boat when I see a woman walking down the ramp to the dock.

It takes a moment to recognize Ruth as she approaches our table wearing a white polo and blue jeans with boat shoes. I stand. "Fancy seeing you here."

She feigns a friendly smile and looks at the group. "Hope you don't mind if I steal Steve for a few minutes. We need to talk."

Her smile disappears when she looks at me. "Where do you want to go?"

I try to ignore Kim's suspicious look. "Let's get a cup of coffee," and gesture back down the dock.

"Sounds good to me," and Ruth turns back to the group. "Nice to meet you."

I want to talk in a public setting, so we walk to the Fisherman's Wharf Inn and order coffee at an outside table.

Ruth's green eyes drill into mine like lasers. "What can you tell me?"

I shake my head. "Nothing more than Brian said on Sunday. The deal is off."

She frowns. "Sunday?"

"Yes. Brian called O'Donnell on Sunday."

Her green eyes turn cold. "I'm no fool. This has something to do with your due diligence report. I need to tell Carson if we have a problem at Beta."

"Tango is my client, not Alpha."

Her eyes don't waver. "You spent a lot of time examining sales reports from London. Why do I think we have a problem in London?"

Our server arrives with our coffee. I stand and say, "Enjoy your coffee."

Ruth shakes her head and says, "You can't just walk away from this – it's not over."

I toss a twenty on the table and say, "Enjoy your coffee."

I pass Kim on the dock as she's leaving the marina for the day. "I hope that woman was business."

28

I retrieve my wine glass from the picnic table and return to Paradox. I email Sarah and exhale a sigh of relief when I see my phone flash *Picasso* a few minutes later.

Sarah asks, "What's up? Any more reaction from Beta?"

"Yes, and I'm baffled. Ruth followed up with more messages today and I just had a personal visit."

"Interesting. What did you say?"

"Nothing about sales. She frowned when I mentioned Brian called O'Donnell on Sunday. From her expression, I'm sure she didn't know O'Donnell waited a day to call Fullerton. There's a lot of internal intrigue in that organization."

Sarah asks, "Does Ruth know Brian told O'Donnell you couldn't verify sales in London."

"I don't think so, but she suspects something is wrong in London. 'This isn't over' were her last words to me."

"What do you want me to do?"

"Nothing at the moment. Just listen. You're the only person I can talk to."

# # #

I've moved to my aft deck with a fresh glass of Chardonnay when Jeff pulls up to the dock. I say, "You're working late."

"Wicked afternoon. A yacht got tangled up in a lobster pot just as I was heading home. I played tugboat to keep it from drifting into boats in the mooring field." He continues, "Thought I would stop by and share the news before I call it a day."

"What news?"

"The medical examiner released the results of the autopsy."

"Drowning?"

"No. They call it suspicious. Owen Clark is the investigator, and he's coming back tomorrow."

I frown. "Why suspicious?"

"Clark said the guy didn't drown. He wants me to prepare a list of every boat in the harbor the day the guy died." He hesitates and says, "He wanted to know if you were still in town. Why were you so interested in the guy's laptop?"

"Just doing a favor for a client."

Jeff pushes off from the dock. "You'll need a better story for Clark tomorrow."

# # #

Amanda calls after dinner. "How was your day?"

"Strange, I wish we could talk about it. How do you like working in Portland?"

"I have mixed feelings. It's easy to work from my desk in the apartment and I love my view of our waterfront. It's easier to do my morning run in Portland, but I prefer to work with our team in person." She pauses, "The best part is being closer to you and Paradox. I miss working with you and look forward to seeing you every weekend."

"I miss you too."

29

I'm walking down the ramp with my Wednesday morning latte when I spot a new face with Kim and Jeff at the picnic table. Jeff stands as I approach and says, "This is Owen Clark, the state's investigator."

Clark stands and I extend my hand. "Good morning, I'm Steve Wilson."

Clark ignores my hand and says, "Is there somewhere private we can talk?"

"Sure." I gesture to Paradox. "Is my boat OK?"

Clark picks up his coffee and follows me to Paradox. He remains standing inside my salon. "I worked with Amanda before she joined the FBI. I'm aware of your relationship."

"Good. How can I help?"

"Michaud's family and firm all want to believe his death was a drowning accident." Clark looks me in the eye. "Michaud didn't drown."

"What happened?"

"He died from a blow to the back of his head. The medical examiner thinks he was killed."

I sit speechless on the edge of my settee.

Clark pulls out a notepad and sets his phone on my small table. "I have a few questions and, with your permission, I plan to record our conversation."

"No problem. Have a seat."

Clark sits in my desk chair and continues staring straight at me. "Steve Wilson, your name keeps coming up in my investigation. I understand you took over Michaud's business assignment and hired a diver to recover his laptop."

"That's correct."

Clark asks, "How were you acquainted with Mr. Michaud?"

"We never met. I arrived in Boothbay Harbor Friday afternoon after his body was discovered."

"Where were you Thursday night?"

"I was on my boat at the Front Street Shipyard in Belfast."

"Was anyone with you?"

"No."

"Can you provide a witness who can confirm you were in Belfast?"

I don't want to sound defensive and pause to consider my answer. "I don't know. The marina's security cameras might confirm my presence. Why?"

"Do you have a car in Belfast?"

"No."

"Do you have access to a car in Belfast?"

"Occasionally. The marina has a vehicle that can be reserved by guests."

Clark continues writing. "Tell me about Michaud's assignment?"

"He was conducting due diligence for a client considering a potential acquisition. His client's investment banker called me after Michaud's accident – sorry, after his body was discovered."

"Why did you search his boat and hire a diver to look for his computer bag and laptop?"

"Michaud's client asked me to complete his assignment. His notes and report were not on the accounting firm's office system. I hoped to find them on his boat or recover them on his laptop."

"Why did you want his report?"

"I thought his notes and report would help me with completing my assignment."

"Did you try to open his laptop and search for his report?"

"No. I placed his case and laptop in a trash bag. I asked Jeff for your contact information and sent them to you."

"Why? We hadn't announced my investigation."

"Just being careful. The medical examiner hadn't released his report."

"How much have you been paid to replace Michaud?"

"I haven't submitted my bill, so I haven't been paid anything."

Clark continues. "Describe this due diligence assignment."

"That might be a problem. I've signed a non-disclosure agreement related to the assignment."

"Why did you sign an NDA?"

"It's standard practice. Firms involved in acquisition negotiations don't want their discussions leaked prior to a public announcement of their transaction."

Clark flips to a fresh page on his notepad and says, "I need the names of people involved in these discussions."

"Sorry, not without checking with an attorney. I suspect you might need a court order."

He frowns. "I hoped you would cooperate. That's all for now, but I'll have more questions."

He reaches for his phone and clicks off the recording. He grins. "Michaud's widow granted access to Michaud's phone and travel records. I really don't need your help."

I'm perplexed by his hostile attitude. "Sorry I can't

be more helpful. I understand you're investigating a possible crime and need to ask questions. Were you able to open and view any files on Michaud's laptop?"

Clark bristles. "That's privileged information, and you are not a participant in my investigation. Thanks for your time."

30

Clark's attitude and questions confuse me. So, I take a bike ride to ponder my next move. When I return, I email Sarah and call Brian.

"Have you heard the results of Michaud's autopsy?"

Brian responds. "No. I thought he drowned in a boating accident."

"That's what I thought, but the medical examiner says Michaud died from a blow to his head and they've classified his death as suspicious. I received a visit from Owen Clark, the investigator, an hour ago."

"Damn." Brian asks, "Was it a robbery?"

"I doubt it. When I searched his boat, I discovered several hundred dollars in cash in his boat's navigation station. I think the only thing missing was the laptop my diver recovered."

"What do they think happened?"

"The state's investigator was probing a connection to Michaud's due diligence assignment."

Brian says, "That seems like a stretch. What do you think?"

"We can't rule it out. He wants the names of the people involved. I said I had an NDA and would need to consult a lawyer. He wasn't pleased with my answer. He has access to Michaud's phone records, so you and Parker should expect phone calls."

Brian says, "Damn. This deal is getting weird. Did you learn anything more about Michaud's death?"

"It's a strange case. He died from a blow to the back of his head and Clark said the medical examiner doesn't think it was an accident. Michaud's dinghy was tied to his sailboat and the swim ladder was lowered for boarding. The police originally assumed he slipped and was unable to board the boat. My diver found Michaud's laptop in the area around the boat, so he could have dropped it if he slipped and fell into the water. Michaud was wearing his life jacket and the incoming tide prevented his body from washing out to sea."

Brian asks, "Why don't they think Michaud hit his head when he fell in the water?"

"I don't know. If he was killed, then the killer didn't need Michaud's dinghy to return to shore. Maybe he had a visitor with another dinghy. They could have argued and Michaud was tossed overboard to look like an accident."

"You really think Michaud was killed?"

"That's why there's an investigation."

"Unbelievable. I can't believe it's related to our due diligence."

"Like I said. We can't rule it out."

# # #

My call from *Picasso* flashes on my phone an hour later. "How's my timing? You said to wait an hour."

"Perfect. I had a curious visit from Detective Owen Clark this morning. The medical examiner has classified Michaud's death as suspicious. He died from a blow to his head and Clark is exploring links to Michaud's due diligence assignment."

"Why? Do you think it's related to the due diligence assignment?"

"It wasn't robbery."

"Did Clark ask you to help with his investigation?"

I laugh. "No. He didn't ask me to help. He treated me like a suspect during our visit."

"Humm .... What would you like me to do?"

"Snoop around Michaud's death. If it's related to Michaud's due diligence work, then it's most likely related to our suspicions of fraudulent activity in London. Dig deeper on Fullerton, Ruth, O'Donnell, Miller, and Earl Baxter."

"Why Baxter?"

"Just curious. He clammed up when I asked about his visit with Michaud."

31

My daily visits to Red Cup are an excuse for a break and a short walk. Thursday morning, I return to enjoy sipping my latte with Kim and other marina friends at the picnic table. Kim says, "Nice to see you back on the dock. It was strange to see you acting like an unsociable hermit. Amanda's a wonderful influence."

I smile and raise my coffee cup in a toast. "Yes, that she is."

Kim says, "You must have been working on something really important. I've never seen you be such a recluse."

I respond. "It was a complex case I needed to finish by July 4th. It was more complex than I expected, but it's finished. I plan to return to my daily bike rides, and Amanda's coming again this weekend. I'm even thinking about a new story and might start writing my next murder mystery."

# # #

Brian calls after lunch. "Clark called me a few minutes ago."

"What did he say?"

"Very formal. He asked if we could discuss

Michaud's assignment. I said I couldn't discuss the assignment without clearance from our lawyers."

"What was his reaction?"

"He hoped we would cooperate without a court order and would get back to me."

"Have you talked to Parker and the attorneys?"

"Yes. Parker and I talked to the attorneys earlier today. They don't want our discussions with Beta to become public and want us to wait until we receive a court order. They plan to request all questions in writing so they can review our answers. This also includes you."

"Humm ...... that's what I expected, but Clark won't like our lack of cooperation."

"We know. I shared your concerns with the attorneys, but they're concerned about disclosing your findings. They will call you in a few minutes."

"Now?"

"Yes, I'm going to hang up and text them."

My phone flashes a new call a few minutes later. "Mr. Wilson, my name is Larry Sanders. I'm the lead attorney for Tango and will help you deal with this investigation into Michaud's death. We plan to cooperate with the investigation, but want to protect you and Tango from any potential legal action. If you accept our representation, then attorney-client privilege protects our discussions."

"I understand. What do you want to know?"

"Do you have a written analysis that supports your opinion about suspicious activity at Beta?"

"Yes. I have a detailed analysis with exhibits outlining my concerns. I have not shared my written analysis with Brian or Parker. O'Donnell didn't let me make copies of any documents. My analysis is based on my notes. As a result, I don't have any documented evidence."

"I'd like to review your analysis."

"No problem. I'll email it to you."

"Do you think Michaud's death is related to his due diligence assignment?"

"I can't rule it out."

Sanders says, "What a mess. Your suspicions about potential illegal payments and accounting fraud are concerning. I advise you to keep avoiding any contact with the people at Alpha and Beta."

"What do I do about future visits from Ruth?"

"You've been advised by counsel not to talk to anyone at Alpha or Beta."

32

Amanda arrives this evening, so I ride my bike to Hannaford's Friday morning, to provision for our weekend. The backpack's straps dig into my shoulders as I walk the bike back down the ramp to Paradox.

Kim greets me as I pass her dock office. "Nice to see you out and about with a smile on your face."

I laugh. "Life is better when Amanda comes for the weekend. I need to get tonight's dinner in the refrigerator."

After unloading, I step out on the dock to help Kim with the lines of an arriving yacht. The skipper says "Thanks" and hands me a twenty. "That's the smallest I have. It's up to you to share it with your blonde helper."

"Guess it's your first time here. Kim's the owner," and I hand her the twenty.

She smiles. "Thanks. I'll put it in the coffee fund."

The embarrassed skipper follows Kim to her dock office to check in and I head up the ramp to buy a BLT at Red Cup for lunch. My upbeat mood darkens on my return when I see Ruth sitting alone at Kim's picnic table.

Confronting her is unavoidable, so I continue down the ramp and walk down the dock toward the table. Ruth stands and feigns her friendly smile. "I stopped in Boothbay to buy you lunch."

I hold up my carry-out box. "You wasted your time. I already have my lunch."

She turns and sits at the table. "I'm not leaving until we talk."

I remain standing. "I have nothing to say. Our attorneys advised me to avoid talking with you."

Ruth's smile disappears and her green eyes turn cold. "Why was Carson contacted by the officer investigating Michaud's death?"

"I don't know."

"Don't know or won't say?"

I remain standing. "I don't know."

She remains sitting. "The investigator said Michaud died under suspicious circumstances. Newspaper articles say his body was found floating in this harbor." She glances towards Kim's dock office. "This is a small town. You must know more."

"Ruth, I have nothing more to say," and walk to my back deck and step aboard Paradox. I'm relieved when Ruth doesn't follow me.

I step out on the dock an hour later and stop at Kim's office door. "I'm headed to Red Cup for an afternoon coffee. Need anything?"

She turns from her computer. "I don't like that woman. Her friendly smile is just an act."

"You're perceptive." I smile. "Need anything?"

"No. Enjoy your walk."

# # #

My attitude improves after a long walk and I read an email from *Picasso* when I return to Paradox.

Steve

Sorry. I'm not learning much additional information about Fullerton or Miller. My agreement with the witness protection program restricts my activity to public documents.

I've relied on your notes about Ruth and O'Donnell. You know they have similar employment contracts and their base pay is identical. Both received the same annual bonus from Alpha for the past five years. Property records show Ruth purchased her condo in an exclusive downtown waterfront building in Boston shortly after joining Alpha.

Your notes show O'Donnell started receiving a second bonus from Beta shortly after Miller came to Palm Beach. He purchased his six-acre estate in West Palm Beach shortly after receiving the first bonus payment.

Baxter joined the accounting firm as a trainee upon graduation from the University of Florida in 1980. He was promoted to managing partner of the Palm Beach office fifteen years ago. He serves on numerous civic and charitable boards and his photo frequently shows up on local society pages. His firm announced plans for his retirement earlier this year.

Michaud graduated from the University of Florida and started his career with the same firm in Palm Beach in 1975. In 1985, Michaud accepted a job with a different firm in Boston and retired two years ago. Baxter and Michaud worked together at the same office in Palm Beach for five years.

Sarah

# # #

Amanda startles me when she steps aboard Paradox at five o'clock. She laughs. "You were deep in thought. Have time for a kiss?"

I jump up from my deck chair. "Absolutely!"

She's still laughing when we separate. "I think you're glad to see me. Let me put my backpack in the salon and let's get a glass of wine."

I'm laughing now. "Damn right. I bought swordfish to grill and we have a bottle of Sauvignon Blanc."

We return to the aft deck with our wine and Amanda says, "A toast to our weekend."

We are both quiet for a minute before she turns. "Rumor has it you had a visit from my former colleague, Owen Clark. Can I ask how you're related to his investigation?"

"Sure. Last weekend, I told you my predecessor on the due diligence project had an accident on his sailboat out in the harbor. He died from a blow to the back of his head and the medical examiner thinks he was killed. Clark is investigating."

She frowns. "I was senior to Clark, and he didn't like working for a woman. I understand he's been asking about our relationship."

I shrug. "He mentioned our relationship during our visit. He seems to think Michaud's death is related to his due diligence assignment."

She's still frowning. "Do you think it's related?"

"I don't know."

33

Amanda prepares pancakes and bacon for breakfast Saturday morning on the aft deck. After breakfast, we take a mid-morning walk to admire sculpture in an art gallery.

I smile. "It's a beautiful day. Let's take a dinghy ride over to the Lobster Pound for lunch this afternoon."

"That's a wonderful idea."

We take a long walk before heading back down to the marina.

Kim frowns and points toward my aft deck as we pass her office. Our pleasant morning comes to an abrupt halt when I spot Ruth sitting in my deck chair.

I'm speechless and Ruth says, "Sorry to interrupt. We need to talk. I'm not moving out of this chair until we do."

Amanda squeezes my arm. "I'll take a walk."

I step aboard and remain standing.

"Carson wants answers, and I'm being stonewalled by O'Donnell and Miller. What did you uncover and why is the deal dead? What does this have to do with Michaud's death?"

I cross my arms across my chest. "Ruth, our attorneys say I'm not at liberty to discuss what I uncovered or why the deal is dead."

"You mentioned Brian called O'Donnell on Sunday. Did Brian give O'Donnell a reason?"

I hesitate to answer but reply. "Yes"

"Is that why O'Donnell waited until Monday to tell Carson?"

"I don't know."

"I believe we have a serious problem. I think you know the answers and I need some direction."

I remain standing on my aft deck with my arms crossed.

She flashes her green eyes and raises her eyebrows. "I'm not moving."

"You were tracking my research on your laptop in Palm Beach."

She says, "I'm not an auditor and don't know what you found in London. Where do I look? I need guidance."

"Ask Baxter to do a special audit. He's your accountant. That's all I have to say."

She stands and steps to the dock. "Thanks. That's a start."

On impulse, I say, "One more thing. Look at the names in Beta's bonus pool."

She gives me a curious glance as she walks away.

I wait a minute before stepping on the dock to look for Amanda. Kim steps out of her office. "She went for a walk and asked me to call her when the coast was clear."

"Thanks. I'll call her."

Amanda is walking down the dock before I place my call. She's not smiling as she approaches.

"I was having a beer up at McSeagull's and saw your friend leave. I hope she was business."

"Her name is Ruth Simpson. She's related to the due diligence investigation."

"Anything you can say?"

"It's a mess and I'm sorry I ever got involved."

Amanda smiles and winks at Kim. "We won't let her spoil our weekend."

34

Paradox feels empty after Amanda heads to Portland early Monday morning. I take my morning walk and stop at Red Cup for a latte on my way back to the marina.

I'm surprised to see Clark talking with Kim when I walk down the ramp. He stands as I approach and I ask, "How's your investigation?"

"Let's talk." He looks at Kim. "We need privacy."

I gesture to Paradox. "Welcome aboard."

He walks to my aft deck and steps aboard.

"Would you like coffee? I have a fresh pot in the galley. I just picked up a latte."

Clark plops down in a deck chair. "How did you know the winch handle was from Michaud's boat?"

"I didn't. The diver found it below the boat, and I previously noticed an empty winch handle pocket in the boat cockpit. It was a last-minute decision to put it in the bag." I pause. "How do you know it came from Michaud's boat?"

Clark ponders his answer. "Forensics found his blood on the winch handle."

"Damn."

Clark shifts in the chair and looks up at me. "Would you sit down?"

"Sure."

Clark leans forward and rubs his temples. He sighs and says, "I may need your help."

"I'll help if I can. Remember, I still have an NDA."

"I remember. So far, everybody tells me the same damn thing. We classified my investigation as suspected homicide this morning. I hope the judge will be more helpful and I can start getting some answers."

I say, "You've been contacting people, so you must have access to Michaud's phone records."

Clark says, "His widow wants answers and gave me his phone and passcode. It's been helpful, but everyone is hiding behind this damn NDA."

He stands and steps back on the dock.

# # #

Brian calls an hour later. "Clark called to tell me Michaud's death is now suspected homicide. What the hell is going on?"

"I wish I knew. He paid me a personal visit about an hour ago."

# # #

I'm feeling frustrated and isolated from Clark's homicide investigation. I worked closely with Mark at the FBI during my banking career and today's consulting agreement between Paradox-Research and Mark's Financial Crimes Unit allows me to work directly with Amanda and other FBI Agents. I don't like being excluded.

35

I'm visiting with friends at Kim's picnic table Tuesday morning when I spot Ruth approaching on the dock.

She feigns her friendly smile and says, "Sorry to drop in without calling. I don't want to leave a trail to my visits."

Her comment leads to suspicious looks from my friends and I say, "Let's get a cup of coffee."

We walk to Fisherman's Wharf Inn and select a waterside table on the outside deck. Ruth was cautious climbing the ramp and winces when she carefully settles into her chair.

"Are you OK?"

"Yeah. Just a few bruises from an unfortunate encounter." Her green eyes focus on mine. "I'm getting stonewalled. Baxter says they've already conducted their regular audit and a special audit would be a waste of time. I saw nothing unusual with the bonus pool information O'Donnell sent me. What am I missing?"

I frown. "You knew O'Donnell was getting a second bonus from Beta?"

Ruth's complexion changes to match her red hair.

She is silent for a minute and asks, "Who can I trust?"

"I don't know."

She turns her gaze to look over the harbor and remains deep in thought. She finally turns back to me. "Carson wants answers. Would you help me if I convince him to hire you?"

"I'm not sure that's his decision."

She grins. "Give me a minute," and she walks to the end of the deck to make a call. She returns in a few minutes and says, "I hope you're right. Carson didn't know O'Donnell receives bonus payments from Miller. He said if it's true, I can hire you to help me."

She slowly stands. "Thanks for the coffee. Please consider my offer. I'll stop by again tomorrow."

I'm stunned and my coffee turns cold while I gaze out over the harbor. I'm startled when my server asks, "Something wrong with the coffee? Your friend didn't touch hers and yours is cold. Do you want a fresh cup?"

"No, thank you. Everything's fine. Here's my credit card."

# # #

I head back to the marina and my friends at the picnic table say, "You look troubled – who is she?"

I answer, "Business problem."

Once aboard Paradox, I email Sarah.

Another visit from Ruth. Please call me.

My phone flashes *O'Keefe* a few minutes later and Sarah asks, "What's up?"

"Ruth's being stonewalled. She says Carson wants answers and wants me to help her."

"That would put you in a tricky situation. Is he willing to let you report illegal financial activity?"

"I haven't discussed arrangements with Ruth or Fullerton. Ruth was spying on my computer research in Palm Beach. I don't know who to trust."

"It's time for you to talk to Mark. You guys worked on investigations for over twenty years while you were chief auditor at the bank. Maybe it's time for him to activate your consulting agreement with the FBI."

"I wanted to wait until my due diligence assignment was over. Tango is clean, but the NDA makes it difficult to share my concerns about Beta."

Sarah says, "Our NDA is with Tango. Why not ask Parker's permission for you to share our findings with Mark?"

"Not that simple. The NDA with Tango restricts sharing information about Alpha and Beta. Tango's attorneys never contemplated a need for me to report suspicious activity at Beta."

"Mark and Amanda are both attorneys. Can you ask their advice on a 'no name' basis?"

# # #

It's time for a long bike ride to help clear my mind and consider my alternatives. I send a text to Mark when I return to Paradox.

Please call me when you have a few minutes to discuss a potential problem.

Steve

An hour later, I see my phone flash *Mark Bouchard* and he says, "I'm always curious when you want to discuss a potential problem. What's up?"

"I'm in a tricky spot and need some advice on a 'no name' basis."

"Steve, we've worked on cases together for over twenty years. You know I can't suppress information concerning a crime."

"I've identified some suspicious transactions and if I uncover criminal activity, it will be reported."

"What's your problem?"

"I uncovered the suspicious activity during a due diligence assignment of an acquisition target we call Beta. My NDA restricts my ability to share information on any of the firms. The suspicious activity is not related to my client. Beta has not produced copies of the transactions in question, and I don't have sufficient evidence for you to open an investigation."

"You're in a tough spot. Are you going to propose a solution?"

"The chairman of Alpha, the private equity firm that owns Beta, has offered to hire me to investigate. My thought is to amend my NDA and due diligence agreements to permit me to report my findings to the chairman of Alpha. If I uncover illegal activity, the agreement will require the chairman to report my findings to the FBI."

I pause and ask, "Does this sound reasonable to you?"

"Do you trust the chairman of Alpha?"

"No. That's why I will add a provision requiring me to report any suspected illegal activity to the FBI if he doesn't comply with our agreement."

"Steve, my job is to uncover and prosecute financial crime. Make certain I'm informed if your investigation uncovers illegal financial activity. Stay safe."

It's time to discuss my plan with Parker and Tango's attorneys. I need their approval to proceed.

36

Yesterday afternoon's discussions with Parker and Tango's attorneys prepare me for today's visit from Ruth. Mid-morning, I see her start down the ramp to the dock and excuse myself from the morning coffee group at Kim's picnic table to intercept her.

"Let's go back to the hotel deck to talk."

She turns and I follow her back up the steep ramp. When we reach the top, I ask, "You're still walking with a limp. Are you OK?"

She frowns, "Yeah. Just taking longer to recover than I expected."

"Can I ask what happened?"

"No. It was just an unfortunate encounter that he'll regret. None of your business."

Ruth gets comfortable at the table and asks, "Have you considered my offer?"

"I have a proposal for you to consider," and hand Ruth a copy of the amendment to my agreements.

Her green eyes sparkle. "Give me a minute."

She stands and blurts out, "Shit!"

Ruth is looking over my shoulder toward the Public Landing and I turn to see a man in black disappear into the crowd.

She frowns. "I'll be back," and she walks to the end of the deck to make a call.

Ruth is grinning when she returns to our table. "Carson has agreed to your proposal. When can you start and what do you need?"

"Answers to some questions before I sign the amendment. Do you trust Carson Fullerton?"

Ruth shrugs. "Not entirely. Carson is motivated to sell Beta and wants to know why you wouldn't issue a clean due diligence report." She pauses and asks, "Do you trust me?"

I shrug. "Not entirely. Who told you to shadow my research at the hotel?"

"That was my decision. I haven't told anybody."

"Why did you unlock the door and come into the suite with a bottle of Champagne?"

"I was bored. I read *Prospère Puzzle* on our flight and was curious. You had been so damn proper and I thought it might break the ice." She pauses. "It was personal, not business."

I ponder her answer and ask, "What's your role at Alpha?"

"Carson hired me to be his buffer. He talks tough but doesn't like to be confrontational. My primary role is to deal with bad news. I'm not popular and know I'm called Ruthless when we make management changes."

"Have you or Carson talked with Owen Clark, the state's investigator?"

"Yes. We understand he thinks Michaud was killed by a blow to the back of his head. Any more questions?"

I push the amendment on the table in her direction. "Carson signs first. Make certain he understands it requires him to report any suspicious activity to the FBI."

"I'll call you after Carson signs."

I stand and say, "Be careful, we don't know if Michaud's death is related to his due diligence findings. He was killed the night before he planned to meet with Fullerton."

Our server reappears and asks, "Are you ready for your check?"

"Yes, but please freshen my cup." I sit down and say, "I'm not in a hurry."

# # #

I'm finishing a bowl of clam chowder for lunch when my phone flashes *Ruth Simpson*.

"Carson signed your amendment and he wants to meet with you this afternoon on his yacht in Camden."

"I don't have transportation."

"No problem. I'll drive down. See you in an hour."

I email Sarah and call Parker to report Fullerton's agreement to my proposal and his request for another meeting on the yacht. I suppress a grin when I read the text from *Picasso*.

Don't plan on eating!

Ruth is quiet on our drive to Camden, and Walt is nowhere in sight when we climb the ladder to the deck of the yacht. Fullerton stands as we approach the aft deck and greets me with a broad smile and firm handshake.

He says, "Welcome aboard. We'll treat you a little better than your last visit. Have a seat. I hope a glass of French Chardonnay is acceptable."

"Thank you, but I prefer ice tea."

Ruth looks at Fullerton. "Warned you."

He chuckles and says, "That you did." We all take a seat at the table and he turns to me. "I'm pleased you accepted my invitation to help us investigate Beta's financials. What can you tell me today, and what do you need?"

"I want to be clear you understand you've hired Paradox-Research to conduct this investigation and our agreement requires you to report any suspicious activity we uncover to the FBI. If you do not comply, then we will report the activity."

"Ruth made that very clear and my lawyers tell me I need to report any illegal activity to protect myself as a whistleblower. I have signed your amendment." He opens a folder on the table and says, "It's your turn to sign."

I sign two copies, fold my copy, and place it in the inside pocket of my blazer before speaking. "My initial due diligence uncovered two potential problems with customer accounts in Beta's London sales office. We traced suspicious payments to shell companies in countries where government officials are suspected of requiring kickbacks to do business. Any kickbacks we confirm violate the Foreign Corrupt Practices Act."

He looks at Ruth. "Who made those payments?"

"Alpha's financial staff makes all payments."

He turns to me. "You said you uncovered two potential problems."

"Yes. I've identified a group of accounts that appear to be a Ponzi scheme to inflate sales at quarter end."

"Shit! Who knows about these potential problems?"

"Brian Tucker, Vince Parker, Tango's attorneys, and Brian mentioned my concerns to O'Donnell on Sunday."

Fullerton frowns. "Ruth told me O'Donnell waited a day to call me. She also said Miller pays him a bonus from Beta's bonus pool. Is that correct?"

"Yes."

He sighs. "It appears he omitted his name from the list he provided Ruth. This information is very troubling, but I don't want to confront O'Donnell until we have all the facts. What do you need?"

"I need access to all of Alpha's and Beta's accounting records with the ability to make copies of any suspicious entries."

Fullerton turns to Ruth. "You call O'Donnell and tell him I have hired Paradox-Research to investigate Beta's financial reports and, if he wants to remain employed, he will cooperate and provide anything Wilson requests."

He turns to me. "I need a drink." He stands and walks into the salon.

Ruth says, "Thanks. I have calls to make. We have a car waiting to take you back to Boothbay Harbor."

"Is Walt driving?

"No. He's on vacation."

# # #

Amanda calls Wednesday evening. "I hope you're free this weekend. I plan to drive down in time for dinner Friday night."

"I plan to be free, but my due diligence assignment has taken a new twist. I'm not sure where it leads."

Amanda sighs, "It better not screw up our weekend."

37

Ruth calls me late Thursday morning. "I called O'Donnell after you left yesterday and told him Carson hired you to investigate Beta's financial reporting. To put it mildly – he went bullshit and hung up. An hour later, O'Donnell placed a call to Carson and left a message saying Miller is outraged and demands an explanation."

I interrupt. "Are you surprised Miller didn't call directly?"

Ruth laughs. "Not at all. Miller talks tough, but they both avoid direct confrontation. Miller always asks O'Donnell to do his dirty work."

"What happened next?"

"I returned O'Donnell's call and calmly explained he needed to comply with Carson's order or Alpha would have a new CFO. It was clear to O'Donnell that Carson asked me to return the call, and after a hostile exchange, he agreed to give you remote access to all of Alpha's and Beta's accounting records. You will not have the ability to make or change any accounting entries."

I respond, "Thank you. This is completely consistent with my request."

Ruth laughs. "O'Donnell doesn't have much respect

for you. He won't provide any new educational guidance and doubts 'my stupid auditor' can open the accounts on his system."

"What did you say?"

"It was my turn to hang up. Get a pen. Here's the online address, your user's name, and password."

# # #

I'm skeptical O'Donnell provided Ruth with accurate access codes, so I'm pleasantly surprised when, fifteen minutes later, I'm looking at an index of accounting reports on my laptop. However, a few more keystrokes hit a dead end. O'Donnell has not opened access to the underlying accounting entries, and I email Sarah.

My phone flashes *Klimt* within seconds.

She asks, "Any progress?"

"Close, but no cigar. He provided access to the accounting reports, but not the entries we need to investigate. Our amended agreement gives us full access. Can you do a workaround or do I need to contact O'Donnell?"

She chuckles. "Being inside their firewall is a hacker's dream. Give me the codes."

My phone flashes a text from *Klimt* an hour later.

We have access to all of Alpha's and Beta's files. I'll download the documents we need to our secure site. I'll update my analysis over the weekend and have a draft report for you on Monday.

I respond.

Well done! I've contacted the security firm we use in Europe and they are investigating Beta's shipments to and from the warehouse in Dordrecht.

# # #

It's now evening and I'm ready for a break. I start a long walk up the street toward Tugboat Inn and plan to circle back on side streets to the marina. I pause at Boothbay Harbor Shipyard to examine their restoration of the *Ernestina Morrissey*, a 152-foot schooner built in 1894.

I hear footsteps approach and turn to view my visitor. A muscular man dressed in black with a black facemask pushes me back against the railing and says, "You've pissed off some very powerful people. Tell that bitch you were mistaken and stop snooping."

I'm at a physical disadvantage but reply, "The cat's out of the bag. It's too late."

"Fuck you." I feel a sharp pain and gasp for air. I can't speak and sink to my knees.

"You and that bitch need to drop it."

The pain in my ribs blurs my vision as I sink to the ground and barf my lunch on the pavement.

"Hey mister. You OK? Should I call an ambulance?"

I gasp, "No, I'll be OK" and see an older couple standing near me as my vision starts to clear.

"Are you sure?"

"I'm just catching my breath. I'll be fine."

I overhear the woman say, "That fool must be drunk," as they walk away.

I stop frequently to catch my breath on my walk back to the marina. I'm grateful the picnic table is deserted and collapse on my settee after gently climbing aboard Paradox.

I'm still on the settee when my phone flashes *Amanda.* Tonight, I ignore her call.

# # #

My voice has lost most of the raspy out-of-breath tone by nine, and I venture a call to Amanda.

She says, "What's wrong? You getting a cold? You sound terrible."

I'm reluctant to tell her about my encounter over the phone and answer, "Just tired. It'll be good to see you tomorrow."

38

Ruth calls Friday morning. "Miller is livid and had a messenger service hand deliver a letter from an attorney to Fullerton an hour ago. The attorney's letter claims Miller's contract gives him full management control of Beta and Fullerton can't interfere in Beta's business. His attorney requested an injunction halting our investigation and a judge in Palm Beach granted an emergency hearing next Tuesday. Fullerton is pissed and hired an attorney to contest Miller's request."

"Miller might have grounds to slow us down. He negotiated a strong contract."

Ruth laughs. "Fullerton can still fire Miller." She pauses. "By the way, O'Donnell called me last night. Miller thinks you are a stupid bank auditor operating out of your depth, and I shouldn't get distracted by your unfounded suspicions."

"What did you say?"

"I said 'thanks for calling' and hung up. Anything new on your end? Did O'Donnell's access codes work?"

"O'Donnell's information was helpful."

"How much time do you need?"

"I'll know early next week."

# # #

Sarah has provided me with access to her workaround, and I download quarter-end sales reports, credits for product returns, and shipping records for the five customer accounts associated with the Dordrecht warehouse.

I'm startled when Amanda steps aboard at five o'clock. I turn in my desk chair and say, "Wow, time got away from me."

"I'm early, you can finish."

"It can wait. I've got all weekend," and slowly stand to greet her with a kiss.

She hugs me and jumps back. "What's wrong? You're in pain. Have you seen a doctor?"

"No. I'm fine. I had an unfortunate encounter."

She gently pulls up my loose t-shirt. "Damn! How did this happen?"

I wince when she touches my ribs. "You need to get an x-ray. I think something's broken. You're coming with me."

An hour later, the emergency room doctor shows us my x-ray with two cracked ribs. "These will heal on their own, but you will be extremely uncomfortable for a couple of weeks. I've ordered a prescription to help with the pain."

Amanda takes the prescription from his hand before I can refuse it. "Thanks. We'll stop at Walgreens on the drive back to the boat."

She helps me back into her SUV. "OK superman. Tell me what happened. This was no accident."

"I told you. I had an unfortunate encounter. We don't need to talk about it."

"Bullshit! I'm not starting this car until you tell me what happened. Were you mugged?"

"No. Someone didn't like my work."

She looks me in the eye for an uncomfortable amount of time, and I feel beads of sweat appearing on my forehead. She breaks the silence by asking, "Is this related to your due diligence assignment?"

I look away. "I can't talk about it."

She persists. "The medical examiner says your predecessor's death wasn't an accident. How dangerous is this assignment?"

"I don't know. Can we please go back to the boat?"

"After we stop at Walgreens."

39

I have a sleepless night and stay in our bunk while Amanda brews coffee and prepares breakfast Saturday morning. She brings me another pill with juice and says, "You look terrible. Take this."

"Thanks for the cheerful greeting. Take it back. I need to stay alert today."

"Humph ...... This must be important. Have you talked to Mark?"

"Yes."

Her stern expression softens. "Whew ..... I feel better. When can we talk?"

"That's up to Mark."

She picks up her phone from the galley counter and makes a call. "Sorry to bother you on a Saturday morning, but I'm looking at a stubborn man with serious bruises and broken ribs. He won't tell me why, but it's related to some dangerous project you know about. One man's already dead and I want to be involved."

She listens for a minute and hands me her phone. "Mark wants to talk to you."

I take the phone and say, "Hi."

"What the hell is going on? You said nothing about this being dangerous. Who's dead? What do I need to know?"

"I'll have the answers next week. That's all I can say for now."

"Your curiosity will get you killed one day. I'm authorizing Amanda to stay with you in Boothbay until we talk next week. Give the phone back to Amanda."

She says, "Thanks," and disconnects.

I pretend to scowl. "Was that necessary?"

She points her finger at me. "Yes. You're stuck with me. Time to get up. Breakfast is ready."

# # #

Amanda's cleaning the galley after breakfast and says, "When you're up to it, let's take a walk."

"Give me a couple of hours. I need to finish my work from yesterday."

"Sounds good to me. I need to check the status of my assignments and decide how to organize working from Paradox."

# # #

Two hours later, she helps me to the dock and I see Kim for the first time since my encounter. She looks at Amanda. "What's wrong with Steve?"

"Damn fool slipped and broke a rib. He'll be OK and

I get to play nurse for a few days."

We turn to depart, and I sigh. "Shit, it's low tide again. I'm not looking forward to climbing ten feet to the top of that ramp."

We stop at the top for me to catch my breath. I momentarily freeze when I spot a man in black sitting at a picnic table in front of the sports bar. I'm relieved when he looks away and remains seated.

# # #

Brian's name flashes on my phone Saturday afternoon. He says, "O'Donnell called me a few minutes ago. Miller wants us to release Beta from our exclusive acquisition negotiations if Tango isn't going to proceed. What do you think?"

"Miller's not the decision maker. I think you should stand pat. Is O'Donnell expecting an answer?"

"Yes. Miller wants either the acquisition agreement or the release signed today."

"Humm …….. You have an exclusive until the end of July. I'd let him simmer and call you back."

Brian laughs. "I agree."

# # #

An hour later, my phone flashes *Brian Tucker*. "O'Donnell didn't wait long. Miller said no more due diligence. We need to shit or get off the pot. Miller has negotiated another acquisition agreement and they're ready to announce the deal tomorrow."

"What did you say?"

"I would inform Parker and our lawyers that Miller intends to breach our exclusive agreement."

"What happened?"

"He hung up. Do you believe they have another deal?"

"No. I think it's a bluff."

# # #

Late afternoon, Amanda returns from Sherman's with a copy of *Prospère Puzzle*. She says, "Please, sign this. Robert arrived today. You promised to give him a signed copy."

She returns a few minutes later. "Robert said 'thanks' and asked if you want to smoke a cigar with him tonight. I told him you cracked some ribs and needed a couple of days to recover from a careless fall."

"Thanks. He's a smart guy. I always learn something new when we discuss investments. I hope to feel up to joining him in a few days."

Amanda frowns. "No other calls this afternoon. Is everything under control?"

"Maybe. I'll know better when I talk to Sarah."

40

I agree to take a pain pill Saturday night. It's hard to find a comfortable position, but I sleep a little better. Sunlight streams into the salon Sunday morning and brightens my outlook for the day. Amanda prepares breakfast and we head for Red Cup after she clears the galley.

# # #

Degas flashes on my phone while we're having lunch on the aft deck. Amanda says, "I'll give you privacy."

I raise my hand. "No. Stay."

Sarah says, "Thought you would like to know Alpha's security service detected our activity on their accounting system. They knew where to look and tried to block our access. O'Donnell must have alerted them."

"What happened?"

"It was a cat-and-mouse game for an hour. They think we're blocked, but we still have total access. I'm almost done."

"Do you expect to see them again?"

"I doubt it. I changed our footprint to a system

their security software doesn't recognize. They won't see us again."

"Thanks for calling. You made my day."

Amanda is smiling when I place my phone back on the table. She says, "That woman is one smart cookie. I'm glad she's on our side today."

I wink. "I thought my call was private."

# # #

We take a nap after lunch. Amanda swings off our bunk after an hour and asks, "How do you feel?"

I suppress a laugh. "Oops. That's not a good idea. It only hurts when I laugh or move."

"You up to a walk? A little exercise might do you good."

"It's not too painful when we go slow. I just need to be careful, but a walk sounds good. I always feel better after a little exercise."

We stop at Red Cup for a couple of lattes and Amanda says, "Show me where you had your unfortunate encounter."

I hesitate. "It was up at the Boothbay Harbor Shipyard. I stopped to look at the *Ernestina Morrissey."*

She smiles. "That sounds like a worthwhile destination. You up for the walk?"

"Sure. Just go slow."

As we pass Tugboat Inn, I say, "Slow down. I can only take shallow breaths and need to stop for a minute."

"Sorry. I'm always in too much of a hurry."

We admire the old schooner's restoration when we arrive at the shipyard, and I'm spooked when I hear footsteps. We both turn and see a man in black approaching.

Amanda steps slightly to one side and removes her backpack as the man approaches me and says, "My friends say you're a slow learner and might need another lesson."

He steps close to me and gestures with his head toward Amanda. "Be a shame if your little blonde friend slipped and broke a rib."

Amanda calmly says, "That would be a mistake."

The man's eyes flare, and he lunges toward Amanda. I hear a gasp and see him crumple to the ground. Amanda removes her badge and Glock from her backpack. He attempts to stand, but freezes when he sees the badge in her left hand and the Glock by her side.

"I'm a Special Agent with the FBI and can arrest you for attempting to assault a federal witness. Take off your facemask and toss your wallet at my feet."

She looks at me. "Take his picture with your phone and take pictures of all the identification in his wallet."

The man glares at me as I snap photos and toss his wallet back at his knees.

Amanda asks, "What do you want to do?"

I can't help but smirk as I see the man's hands grasping below his belt as he rests on his knees in front of Amanda. "Let's send him back with a message." I look down at him. "Tell your friends that train has left the station."

Amanda says, "You can get up and walk away. I don't want to see your face again in Boothbay."

We watch the man slowly limp away and head towards downtown. Amanda puts everything in her backpack and says, "Let's take the long way back. I don't think he's in a rush."

I grin and ask, "What just happened? How did you do that?"

She laughs. "I'm not just a pretty face. We have some training."

"No shit. Remind me to never piss you off."

We walk for a couple of blocks before I say, "That was interesting. He didn't know you're with the FBI."

"Apparently not."

# # #

We make it back to the marina about an hour later and Amanda says, "I need to file a report with Mark saying I displayed my weapon to prevent an assault on a potential witness."

"Thanks. I'm grateful you were with me."

"Right. He could have rearranged your teeth this time." She asks, "Who do you think sent him?"

"I don't know. I'm going to text his photo to Ruth Simpson and email Sarah to do a background check while you call Mark."

Ruth calls me a few minutes later. "I'll be damned. That's Mike, Miller's driver. He wanted me to stop messing around in Miller's business. I'm sorry, I thought it was personal and just directed at me."

I ask, "What happened?"

Ruth says, "He lost his temper when I said 'fuck off' and he hit me in the ribs. Why is Mike on his knees in this photo?"

"He had an unfortunate encounter with Amanda."

She laughs. "Oh. I wish I could have seen that."

# # #

Amanda joins me after she completes her call with Mark. "Learn anything?"

"Yes, but this is awkward. I'm still restricted by my NDA."

She frowns. "So, this is related to your due diligence assignment."

"Yes. I'm waiting to learn more from Sarah."

# # #

Sarah emails me after dinner.

The employment photos and information all match. Your man in black is Mike, Miller's driver. He is also Walt's brother. They both served in the Special Forces in Afghanistan and joined a special security firm in Palm Beach after they were discharged. The file says O'Donnell hired Mike as Miller's driver one week before Walt joined Alpha as Fullerton's driver. Baxter's firm does the audit for the security firm and he recommended both men to O'Donnell. As they say, 'It's a small world.'

41

Amanda's up at six on Monday to take her regular morning run before preparing our breakfast. I put the finishing touches on my report linking shipments back and forth to the Dordrecht warehouse with the offsetting accounting entries.

Sarah posted her detailed report to our secure site earlier this morning. As expected, she has posted accounting entries and wire transfers for the agent commissions paid to shell companies for sales in countries noted for kickbacks to government officials. The money trail for these payments ends at numbered bank accounts in Switzerland, Cyprus, and Malta.

She has also prepared a chart illustrating agent commissions paid for fake sales to the five mystery accounts. These payments all end up in bank accounts owned by another shell company.

My phone flashes *Monet* at eight and I signal Amanda for privacy.

"Good morning, Sarah. Your report and diagrams are excellent. The excerpts from our geopolitical service link these payments to suspected kickbacks to government officials in each of these countries. Your report is more than sufficient for Mark to open an official investigation."

"Thanks. Have you heard from the investigators in The Netherlands?"

"They promised an update today. It's early afternoon in Rotterdam. I'll call Ruth to schedule my meeting with Fullerton once I get their report."

# # #

The lead investigator from Europe calls an hour later. "Sorry, we ran a bit late. We wanted to visit with the second driver this morning to confirm our findings. I've just emailed our report. Here's the highlights."

"First, we matched all the deliveries on your list to specific trucks and drivers. We were lucky. They use a small outfit and two drivers make all the shipments on this route. We completed visits with both drivers this morning?"

"Second, the building in Dordrecht is not a typical warehouse. It has multiple self-storage units like the facilities you have in America. The shipments for all five accounts went to the same storage unit. The unit is rented in the name of a logistical firm that doesn't exist."

"Third, the drivers describe their deliveries as a round-robin. They just move boxes back and forth. They report no shipments made to outside customers."

"Fourth, my agent took several photos while the door to the storage unit was open. These photos confirm the inventory count you suspected. No products have been delivered to outside customers. This is all detailed in our written report."

I say, "Great job!" and ask, "How did you gather so much information over the weekend?"

"Not a problem. The worldwide shortages have all shipping companies working every day. My agents posed as other drivers and just started complaining about being overworked and underpaid. The drivers for these shipments opened up like a can of sardines. My guys know how to take clandestine photos. Your assignment was a piece of cake."

# # #

I add the Dordrecht report to our file, prepare a summary of our investigations, and call Ruth.

"I'm ready to meet with you and Fullerton."

"Anytime. Do you need transportation?"

"No. Amanda will drive me. We can be at the yacht about three."

# # #

Ruth meets me at the boarding ladder, and Fullerton is waiting on the aft deck when I arrive.

Ruth says, "We're serving ice tea today. Have a seat."

They both take seats and I hand each of them an envelope. "This is a summary of our Paradox

Report. We have all the backup exhibits on our secure site. I'll be quiet and let you read our summary."

Fullerton's face matches Ruth's red hair when he finishes and puts our report on the table. "When can I give the full report to my attorneys?"

I push three flash drives across the table. "The full report with exhibits is on these drives. The third drive is for your attorneys. I can also email copies if they have a secure system."

Fullerton passes a business card across the table. "Email him a copy as soon as possible."

I take my laptop out of my case, confirm access to my virtual private network, and email the documents.

Fullerton says, "Our agreement says I have forty-eight hours to review and send your reports to the FBI. I want to review them with my attorney first, but we will send your Paradox Report to the FBI by noon Wednesday."

Fullerton looks at Ruth. "You ask questions. I want to know who's responsible." He stands and says, "I've lost my appetite" and he passes the server coming out with a tray of fresh ice tea as he enters the salon.

Ruth waits until the server departs. "Who's responsible? Your report says what happened, but you don't say who's responsible."

"That's a job for the FBI. Our job was to investigate the transactions, not the people."

Ruth sighs and holds up her flash drive. "I need to read the full report and talk to Carson. You should plan on coming back tomorrow for lunch."

I wave to Amanda from the top of the boarding ladder and take the short walk to her parked SUV. She says, "That was fast."

I smile. "The cat's out of the bag."

42

Camden, Maine

We arrive in Camden Tuesday morning in time for coffee at the Owl and Turtle Bookshop. Amanda grins as I select a pastry.

We find an outside table and I say, "Insurance. I'm hungry and have never been offered something to eat on that yacht."

Ruth greets me at the top of the boarding ladder. Fullerton is seated at the table when we join him on the aft deck. I see ice tea on the table and shrimp pasta arrives before we take our seats.

Fullerton says, "I discussed your Paradox Report with my attorneys yesterday afternoon. They reviewed it with Miller and O'Donnell this morning, and my attorneys sent your report to the FBI."

I ask, "What's the status of Miller's request to the Palm Beach court for an injunction?"

Ruth chuckles. "Miller withdrew his request when Fullerton's attorney said he was prepared to submit the Paradox Report to the judge."

Fullerton smiles. "Ruth can tell you about my

attorney's discussions with O'Donnell and Miller."

Ruth says, "Both deny any knowledge of these activities. Miller says he told O'Donnell to fire those crooks in London. O'Donnell blames Earl Baxter for not spotting the fraudulent activity in his audits." She smirks. "Our attorney said you could lose an eye around those guys with all their finger pointing."

Fullerton looks at me. "Who is responsible?"

"That investigation needs to start at the bottom and work its way up. The signatures on the entries are all accounting or sales clerks. Your executives all attempted to disguise any direct involvement."

Ruth asks, "Will you do that investigation?"

"No. The criminal investigation is a job for the FBI and the authorities in Europe."

Fullerton sighs. "I'm mad as hell, but my attorney tells me I should wait to fire O'Donnell and Miller until we know more about their involvement. A premature termination without solid facts could trigger a lawsuit."

Ruth asks, "Are you willing to share any opinions?"

"No."

Fullerton looks at Ruth. "We have a management problem at Beta and I still want to sell the company." He turns to me. "Do you have any suggestions?”

“I’m not your investment banker. I suggest you have O’Donnell contact Brian Tucker.”

Fullerton’s face turns red. “Bullshit.” He turns to Ruth. “You call Brian Tucker.”

Ruth says, “That will piss off O’Donnell and Miller.”

“Good! You tell them I’ve delegated all negotiations to you.” Fullerton looks at me. “Enjoy your lunch. I need to talk to my attorney.”

Ruth smiles. “We can finish lunch. I’ll make my calls this afternoon.”

I ask, “Have you told Carson about your encounter with Miller’s driver?”

“Not yet. Should I?”

“That’s up to you.”

# # #

I wave to Amanda and walk to her SUV. She says, “Were you served lunch today?”

I grin. “Yes. Finally. We can go across the harbor so you can eat before we head back to Boothbay. I’ll order coffee and some blueberry pie.”

We find an outside table at Peter Ott’s and laugh as we revisit the cruises we’ve had to Camden on Paradox. Amanda's phone buzzes halfway through lunch. "It's Mark."

She stands and walks to a private spot at the railing overlooking the harbor. I watch her shake her head, look my direction, and return to the table.

She smiles. "Mark received copies of your report from Alpha's attorneys about an hour ago. Their letter says the Paradox Report is being submitted under the 'whistleblower provision' to protect Carson Fullerton and Ruth Simpson from prosecution. Mark designated me as agent in charge of our investigation."

I lift my glass of ice tea to toast. "That's the best news I've heard in weeks!"

"I'll read your report this afternoon. I'm not sure when we can talk about the case. Mark says we need to clarify your role as a potential witness."

# # #

Tuesday night, we walk hand-in-hand across the footbridge to Coastal Prime to celebrate Amanda's involvement with a glass of Champagne and a lobster dinner.

43

Boothbay Harbor, Maine

I'm busy Wednesday morning on my aft deck catching up with my regular quarterly activities for existing clients when Amanda says, "Please, come inside when you're finished."

"Mark says your agreement with Alpha requires your full cooperation and I need to view you as a cooperating witness. He does not plan to activate your consulting agreement. I'm just going to take notes today. At some point, we will record a deposition. Are you ready?"

"Sure"

"Today, I want background on the people involved. How would they benefit from Beta's fraudulent activity? Let's start with Carson Fullerton."

"Fullerton has unhappy investors and wants to sell Beta. The fraudulent sales will increase Beta's acquisition price. His cooperation could be a coverup to disguise his knowledge of Beta's scheme. His attorney is seeking to protect him as a whistleblower."

"How about Patrick O'Donnell?"

"O'Donnell's staff completes all of Alpha's and Beta's financial transactions at Alpha's office in Palm Beach. He's the contact for acquisition negotiations and due diligence. He did his best to prevent my analysis of Beta's sales. Miller pays him a special bonus from Beta that could be a payoff. Fullerton says he was not aware O'Donnell was receiving bonus payments from both Alpha and Beta."

"Max Miller?"

"Miller's employment contract provides for a substantial bonus when Beta is sold. He has the most to gain from the fraudulent sales and a high acquisition price. He authorized the special bonus from Beta to O'Donnell. He hired the new sales team in London." I pause. "His driver assaulted both Ruth and me."

"Ruth Simpson?"

"She works for Fullerton and her relationship with O'Donnell and Miller appears to be hostile. Her involvement started when Tango hired me to complete due diligence. She says her assignment is to expedite the sale of Beta to Tango. She was shadowing my due diligence research on her laptop in Palm Beach. Fullerton asked her to find out why I wouldn't issue my due diligence report."

"Earl Baxter?"

"Baxter's firm issues financial statement audits for both Alpha and Beta. Junior staff at the firm's London office did the audit work for Beta's foreign sales. He plans to retire at year-end and this investigation will be a black mark on his record."

Amanda pauses. "What about the drivers?"

"Someone told Miller's driver to confront both Ruth and me. He tried to stop our investigation of Beta's London office. Miller is the obvious culprit, but maybe too obvious. They all had reasons to halt my due diligence and we also can't rule out one of the unhappy foreign investors."

Amanda closes her laptop and says, "I'm sorry we let Mike go."

"It didn't make any difference. He would have been out on bail the same day. Ruth says Walt is on vacation and he hasn't returned to Fullerton's yacht."

Amanda says, "It's time to have an agent in Palm Beach visit Mike."

She shrugs. "This entire investigation is upside down. It's better when our suspects don't know what we know. Our suspects have copies of your report and time to cover their tracks."

I say, "If everyone wants to look innocent, then they might agree to informal visits to help you with the investigation. Cooperating will allow them to claim innocence and point fingers."

"Good idea. I'll start making some phone calls."

44

Camden, Maine

Thursday morning, Amanda is driving as we head to Camden for her visits with Ruth and Fullerton. She explains. "I want to keep today's visits informal, but I will explain their legal rights and ask permission for you to attend. They might ask you questions, but I don't want you to answer or ask questions. Don't speak unless I ask you a question. I only want you to observe and remember any inconsistencies."

We approach the boarding ladder of Fullerton's yacht at a quarter after nine. Amanda shouts up to the young woman on deck. "Hi. I'm Amanda Smith with the FBI. I have a meeting with Ruth Simpson at nine-thirty."

Ruth appears at the railing. "Welcome aboard."

Amanda is first up the ladder. "Hi. I'm Amanda Smith."

Ruth smiles. "I've read Steve's books. I thought you were a fictitious character until I saw you at the marina. Blonde ponytail, blue jeans, and a small backpack all match your description in his books. So, it's true, you only wear a uniform when you make an arrest?"

"That's right."

"Welcome aboard. Is it OK if we meet on the aft deck?"

"That's fine."

"I'll excuse the crew after she serves coffee, so we will have privacy." Ruth turns to me. "Welcome aboard."

The young woman serves three coffees and assorted pastries after we take our seats at the table. Amanda opens with her legal preliminaries and says, "Thank you for your cooperation. Your help in sorting out this situation is greatly appreciated."

Ruth smiles. "Glad to help. Carson and I want to get to the bottom of this mess. You should know I have contacted Brian Tucker and told him Carson understands we may need to renegotiate the acquisition price to reflect a potential problem. We've extended the exclusive negotiation time with Tango until the end of August. That gives us time to negotiate a price and the terms of the acquisition."

Amanda says, "Thank you for keeping me up-to-date." She asks, "When did you first suspect something might be wrong in London?"

"I was using my laptop to shadow the accounts Steve was investigating during his due diligence visit to Palm Beach. Everything looked fine to me, but I became suspicious when he wouldn't issue his due diligence report."

"Have you discussed the Paradox Report with Fullerton, O'Donnell, Miller, or Baxter?"

"Only with Carson."

"What's your relationship with Carson?"

"It's strictly professional. His wife stays with him on the yacht. He acts tough but avoids confrontation and uses me as his voice with management. I worked on several assignments for Alpha as a management consultant before he offered me a job. I evaluate the management of the fund's investments."

"Did you evaluate Beta's management?"

"Yes. I recommended several strategic changes before Carson hired Miller."

"Did you recommend Miller?"

Ruth pauses. "I didn't object. Carson asked me to review my recommendations with Miller. He asked my opinion of Miller."

"What happened?"

"I'm embarrassed to say Miller made a fool of me. He was very complimentary of my recommendation to add customer support staff to improve quality control and design new products. He lied and said my recommendations provided him with a fantastic roadmap for significant performance improvements at Beta."

"So, what happened?"

"Miller did the opposite. He made across-the-board cost cuts, fired the quality control staff and product development team. He transferred accounting, financial audit, payroll, and his personal expenses to Alpha. Miller is more interested in playing financial games to earn his bonus than building a solid business."

"What do you know about his London sales team?"

"Only what's in Miller's management reports."

"Have you been to Beta's London office?"

"No."

"Do you think Miller knew about London's sales practices?"

"Good question. If he did, you won't find his fingerprints. Miller delegates all his dirty work."

"Who assaulted you?"

"Mike. Miller's driver and security guard."

"Did you inform Fullerton?"

"No. Not yet."

"Why do you think Mike assaulted you?"

"Mike told me to stop snooping around Beta. He lost his temper when I said 'fuck off'."

"Who do you think told him to assault you?"

She pauses. "Miller's the most obvious, but I really don't know. I don't know who to trust."

Amanda says, "Thank you. I'll have more questions as my investigation proceeds. I hope we can rely on your continued cooperation."

Ruth says, "You can."

"We're finished for today. Please tell Fullerton I'm ready for our questions."

# # #

"Mr. Fullerton, thanks for your cooperation. I need to cover a few legal points before we start."

Fullerton grins. "Glad to help. My attorneys assure me I'm protected as a whistleblower, and it's important for me to fully cooperate."

"Have you discussed this investigation with Miller, O'Donnell, Baxter, or Ruth?"

"My only discussions have been with Ruth." He frowns. "I'm furious and want to fire those incompetent fools. I rely on my people to be honest and feel completely violated!"

"Did you know Miller eliminated Beta's audit function?"

"I don't recall. He might have mentioned it in one of his management reports."

"Did you know O'Donnell was receiving a bonus from Beta?"

"No. We caught him double-dipping and I can't wait to fire the two-timing SOB."

Amanda continues. "Who benefits following the acquisition of Beta by Tango?"

Fullerton pauses. "I guess we all would."

"Do you plan to discuss this investigation with Miller, O'Donnell, or Baxter?"

"Yes. I'm mad as hell. But my attorneys told me to wait until your investigation is complete."

"When did you first learn about these suspicious transactions at Beta's London office?"

He gestures at me. "When I read his report."

"Why did you hire Walt?"

He frowns. "Why is that important?"

Amanda smiles. "Please answer my question."

"Miller said we should both have security protection. He suggested O'Donnell arrange for Walt to replace my driver."

"Did you interview Walt?"

"No. He's just a driver and provides protection. I don't get involved in low-level employee matters."

She gestures toward me. "Did you know Miller's driver assaulted Steve and attempted to assault me?"

Fullerton looks at me. "He did what? When? Why?"

Amanda answers, "He said Steve had pissed off some very powerful people and he and that bitch need to stop snooping."

"Damn. Were you hurt?"

Amanda continues. "What's your relationship with Ruth?"

"She's my right-hand man. Smart as a whip and does a great job evaluating my managers and their strategy. I'm a strong and demanding executive and she handles tough assignments for me."

"What's your relationship with O'Donnell?"

He snorts. "Before this fiasco, he managed financial negotiations and investment strategy for me. I'm going to fire him after this is over."

"What's your relationship with Miller?"

"That loudmouth is out of his depth. He doesn't listen to anybody and has screwed me and my fund's investors. We're all pissed."

Amanda tilts her head. "We're all pissed? Have you discussed this investigation with your investors?"

He turns crimson. "No. One of my foreign investors called me to ask what was going on at Beta."

"How did your investor know about this investigation?"

"He said he heard a rumor and it better not screw up his investment."

"Have you told anybody about his call?"

"Of course not! I can't tolerate negative rumors about my funds."

"What are your plans for Beta?"

"Miller screwed everyone. I don't have time to fix it again, so I've asked Ruth to negotiate a deal with Tango. I should never have relied on that two-timing O'Donnell."

"Who suggested the Tango deal be for cash and stock?"

"O'Donnell said it was Miller's idea. If the results don't measure up to his expectations, then we would have the votes to have Tango's board replace Parker."

"Interesting. Who would replace Parker as CEO of Tango?"

"O'Donnell said he could probably convince Miller to fix the combined company."

Amanda says, "That's all for today. I appreciate your candor and cooperation. I'll probably have more questions after I visit with O'Donnell, Miller, and Baxter."

# # #

We stop at Peter Ott's for lunch at a waterfront table. Amanda says, "I don't want to discuss the case until I finish my visits in Palm Beach. I need to keep an open mind."

I say, "Speaking of Palm Beach, we need to start for Bangor in thirty minutes for our flight tonight."

Amanda laughs. "I hope you can endure a coach seat on a commercial flight and a night at the Holiday Inn. My budget doesn't cover a private jet and a suite at The Breakers."

45

Palm Beach, Florida

Amanda's phone chirps Friday morning while we're eating our boxed breakfast in the lobby of the Holiday Inn. She shakes her head. "It's a text from the agent with the Serious Fraud Office in England. He had a warrant to search Beta's London sales office yesterday afternoon. The office was deserted and a shredder was overflowing. They've issued arrest warrants for the three sales executives."

I say, "Humm .... Everyone's trying to cover their tracks."

# # #

I take the lead when we enter Alpha's office building. The receptionist directs us to the conference room with a view of the Intracoastal Waterway and we find coffee and donuts waiting for us.

O'Donnell arrives promptly at nine o'clock. "Hi. I'm Patrick O'Donnell. I see you found the coffee and donuts I arranged. Let me know how I can help with your investigation. We all need to get to the bottom of these sales discrepancies."

Amanda smiles. "I appreciate your willingness to

cooperate. I need to cover some legal points before we start."

When she finishes, she asks, "When did you first learn about these sales discrepancies?"

He gestures to me. "When Fullerton's lawyers sent me his report."

"What is your job at Alpha?"

"I'm the Chief Financial Officer and have responsibility for our investment strategy and acquisition negotiations."

"Who's responsible for Alpha's accounting and financial reporting?"

"I delegate those functions to my staff."

"Who's responsible for Beta's accounting and financial reporting."

"Beta's staff sends electronic accounting entries to my staff for their review. It's a check and balance system. My staff checks the accuracy of each accounting entry before it's recorded on Beta's financial statements."

"What was the process for the London office?"

"It was the same. The people in London sent electronic entries to my staff for their review. I've already held a staff meeting to review the process. All of those entries were processed correctly. My staff is not responsible for confirming customer sales or collecting accounts receivable. That's the responsibility of the staff in London."

"Does Beta have an accounting function?"

"No. Beta transferred accounting to Alpha."

"What's the process for Alpha's entries?"

"It's the same process."

"Who sends the entries to your staff for Alpha's expenses?"

"Oh. Most of Alpha's expenses are routine for items like salary and rent. They just happen, probably like the automatic payment of your electric bill."

"Was your bonus payment from Beta a routine transaction?"

Beads of sweat appear on O'Donnell's forehead.

"Yes. A clerk reviews all bonus agreements, calculates amounts, and makes the payments."

Amanda asks, "Who authorized and signed your bonus agreement?"

"Miller said he asked Fullerton to authorize my bonus. It's paid from Beta's bonus pool, so Miller signed it. Miller said I'm a phenomenal help to his management team and I deserve an extra bonus."

"Does Beta have an audit function?"

"No. Miller said their questions were an insult to

effective management, and he eliminated the function."

"Does Alpha have an audit function?"

"No. I rely on Baxter's audit at year-end."

Amanda stands. "Thank you for your cooperation. I'll have more questions, but this does it for today."

# # #

We take a taxi to Miller's office and arrive ten minutes early. He keeps us waiting for another fifteen minutes before opening his office door. "I'm very busy today. I hope we can keep this short. I need to get to the bottom of this fiasco and fire some more people."

Amanda stands and smiles. "Good morning. I'm Amanda Smith, a Special Agent with the FBI. I'm in charge of the FBI's investigation of Beta's financial activity. I appreciate your willingness to cooperate."

She walks past Miller into his office and takes a seat on the sofa to avoid the glare of sunlight from the window behind Miller's large desk. I follow and take a seat in a chair on the opposite side of the room. I spot Miller's suit coat on a hanger in the open closet.

Miller follows me. "Sit over there so I can see both of you."

I smile. "I'm comfortable here."

He grumbles, slumps into his desk chair, loosens his tie, and puts his feet up on his desk.

He looks at Amanda. "Don't you have a uniform?"

She grins. "I only wear my FBI uniform when I make an arrest."

"Wearing jeans is disrespectful. What can I do for you? Keep it brief. I'm busy."

Amanda shrugs. "We're all busy. I appreciate your cooperation and need to read you a few legal statements before we start."

"Get on with it!"

Amanda reads her statements and asks, "When did you first learn about Beta's suspicious sales transactions?"

"When Fullerton's damn lawyer called me. What a wimp. Fullerton should have called me before this so-called investigation started. Beta is my responsibility. Fullerton and that woman have no right to interfere."

He looks at me. "You should have come to me. I would have fixed any problem and this acquisition would be done."

Amanda asks, "What due diligence did you do on the London sales team?"

He glares at Amanda. "They had an amazing international reputation for increasing sales."

"Who approved the payment of the bonus from Beta to O'Donnell?"

"Fullerton. I was surprised when O'Donnell told me Fullerton approved payments to him from Beta's bonus pool."

Amanda looks puzzled. "Oh. I thought you signed the bonus agreement."

Miller pauses. "I only signed after O'Donnell told me it was Fullerton's idea."

"How do you verify sales and commission payments for accuracy?"

"I'm not responsible for accounting. O'Donnell said he needed to manage the accounting staff for control. That's his job. Fullerton needs to fire him and hire someone competent. O'Donnell's lack of oversight is inexcusable!"

"Who eliminated Beta's audit function?"

"Those green eyeshade idiots are an insult to effective management!" He pauses. "O'Donnell made that decision."

Amanda smiles. "I enjoyed reading your recent magazine interview. The reporter referred to your book describing your turnaround success. I can see why you're called Magic Max."

Miller beams and takes his feet off his desk. He leans forward and smiles at Amanda. "I hate that nickname. My results aren't magic, they're the result of brilliant management."

Amanda frowns. "Why didn't Baxter uncover these suspicious transactions in his annual audit?"

"He's another stupid, green eyeshade, bean counter. He's just coasting until retirement. Fullerton should have fired him years ago."

Amanda stands. "One more thing. What happens with Beta now?"

Miller stands. "I've achieved a fantastic turnaround. This is just a minor distraction and Beta is a very profitable fit with Tango. I'll get this deal back on track. I just hope Parker doesn't screw it up and I have to fix it again."

"Thanks for your time. You've been very helpful."

He follows us and closes the door. Amanda stops and fumbles with her backpack. She looks at Miller's assistant. "Be back in a minute."

She opens the door to Miller's office and I hear him say, "That stupid bitch just left ……"

I see him turn toward the open door and Amanda smiles. "Sorry, one more question. Have you discussed the investigation with your London sales team?"

Miller's face is so red I fear he might pop a blood vessel. "Damn right! I fired the entire bunch yesterday! Get out!"

Amanda smiles and walks to the coffee table. "Sorry to interrupt your call. I forgot my pen."

# # #

Miller's Bentley is waiting at the entrance when we enter our taxi. I turn to Amanda. "That's Miller's car, but that's not his driver."

"I know. Our local agent sent me a text. Both brothers have disappeared."

I ask, "How did you know Miller was on his phone?"

"The light flashed on his assistant's console. I wanted an excuse to return and ask about communications with London. I left my pen on his coffee table. His reaction to my intrusion was priceless."

"He was livid."

Our taxi arrives at Baxter's office building and he is waiting for us in a small conference room.

Amanda greets him with a smile. "Thanks for taking time to visit with me. I need your help, but first, let me get the legal formalities out of the way."

I pour coffee from a carafe on the credenza and find a chair at the end of the table.

Amanda says, "I know your audit reports rely on Beta's internal controls. I'm confused. Who's responsible for Beta's internal controls?"

"Miller has ultimate responsibility at Beta. He signs the internal control statements for our year-end audits."

"Who did the fieldwork for the London office?"

"We have a small staff in London and they send a junior accountant for a routine audit. I review the file to confirm he sampled the appropriate number of transactions. Everything is in order. He found no outages and no customer accounts were past due. Nothing looked suspicious."

"He didn't notice five accounts had no cash transactions?"

"The accounts all balanced and nothing was past due. No red flags."

"What did John Michaud discuss with you the day he scheduled his meeting with Fullerton?"

"It was just a personal visit. He was my mentor and his accident was tragic."

Amanda frowns. "He died under mysterious circumstances. We believe his death is related to his due diligence work." She asks, "What did you discuss?"

Baxter stands and walks to the window. Amanda waits for his answer.

He finally turns. "It was a personal visit about a family matter."

Amanda stands. "Thank you for your time and cooperation. We have a flight to catch."

46

Boothbay Harbor, Maine

We're both tired Saturday after our late arrival in Bangor to retrieve Amanda's SUV and drive to Boothbay. We walk to Red Cup on a foggy morning for lattes after our breakfast of fruit and cereal.

Amanda says, "The fog's lifting, so let's sit over at that picnic table. I need to think about my approach to Clark this afternoon."

"What do you want to accomplish?"

"If he has access to Michaud's phone, then he has access to his laptop. I want to know what Michaud uncovered."

I say, "Michaud's firm is being stonewalled. Clark won't share the laptop's information until they agree to cooperate and the attorneys still want all questions and answers in writing."

Amanda says, "The cat's out of the bag and we need to move fast before this coverup is successful. Both brothers and the London sales team have already disappeared. Everyone else is pointing fingers. I need something I can take to a judge to penetrate this coverup."

#   #   #

We're waiting at Kim's picnic table when Clark arrives at two. Amanda gestures to Paradox and says, "Let's go aboard for privacy."

Clark follows Amanda, and I close the door to the salon behind us. Amanda takes a seat on the settee and I move forward to the navigation station. Clark remains standing.

Amanda says, "Please take a seat. Steve's desk chair is fine."

"I'll remain standing. You said we need to talk. What about?"

"Your investigation of Michaud's death."

"That's my investigation. No need for the FBI to take control."

"Relax. I don't want to take control. It's your case. We might be able to help each other solve a complex crime."

"How?"

"We can start by sharing some information. I'll go first. If you think we can be helpful, then I would like access to the information on Michaud's laptop."

He sits in my desk chair facing Amanda. "You first."

She gestures to me. "Steve uncovered a complex financial fraud during his due diligence.

We suspect Michaud uncovered the same fraud, and it may have been the reason he was killed." Clark leans forward. "Who killed Michaud?"

Amanda shakes her head. "I don't know. We've uncovered accounting fraud, a coverup is underway, and Michaud is dead. Several people had reason to cover up the fraud and their finger pointing is unbelievable."

"How does this help me?"

"Unraveling the coverup should lead you to Michaud's killer. I think the information on Michaud's laptop might lead us to our culprit and your killer."

"Why should I trust you when everyone else is stonewalling me?"

She smiles. "We're on the same side. We both want to solve a crime."

Clark bristles. "I don't want you to take credit for solving my homicide investigation."

"Michaud was killed in Maine. It's your case, not ours. You'll get the credit. What have you learned?"

"Damn little. Everyone on my list has an alibi the night Michaud was killed. Miller, O'Donnell, and Baxter were all in Florida. Fullerton said he was on his yacht with his wife, a crew member, and Walt. Ruth Simpson was in Arizona."

Amanda says, "It's a puzzle. Do you have access to Michaud's due diligence files?"

"Michaud's widow found the code to open his phone and a password for his backup account on the cloud. His phone and laptop both have access to the backup files on his cloud account. However, his widow doesn't know the password he used to protect the file for Tango. We're at a dead-end."

Amanda says, "We could help."

Clark bristles. "I'm not turning Michaud's laptop over the FBI."

I raise my hand. "May I make a proposal?"

They both look my direction and I address Clark. "My firm uncovered Beta's accounting fraud. I will share my firm's report with you if you give me the address to Michaud's cloud account. You have his laptop because I paid a diver to recover it and I voluntarily sent it to you. But I don't need his laptop. My firm has a staff member who should be able to open the files Michaud saved on his cloud account, and I'll share them with both of you."

Clark pauses. "I get your report first. If it's useful, then I'll give you the address of Michaud's cloud account."

I stand up and walk to my desk, pick up a flash drive, and write on a small pad. I hand Clark the flash drive and pad. "This is the password to my report."

I return to the navigation station while Clark removes his laptop from his case. He places the flash drive in the laptop and starts reading.

Fifteen minutes later, he turns and says, "You got a deal" and he writes on the pad. "Here's the address of Michaud's cloud account."

I email the address to Sarah. Amanda and I wait in silence while Clark reads my report.

Thirty minutes later, my phone flashes a text from *Picasso*.

Michaud's due diligence files are on our secure site.

I open our secure site and download Michaud's files to two flash drives. I stand. "His due diligence files are on these drives."

Clark removes my report drive, adds the new drive, and starts reviewing the information.

He stands a few minutes later and says, "Thanks." He turns to Amanda. "Keep your promise. I want credit for this case."

She smiles. "Michaud's death is your case."

# # #

We both start reviewing Michaud's notes and the exhibits he saved in his due diligence file. Amanda says, "Michaud's notes confirm he talked with Baxter about London's sales and his plan to meet with Fullerton. I'm surprised his notes are so tough on his former colleague."

Wednesday 6/16: O'Donnell continues to block my access to London's customer accounts.

Thursday 6/17: Stopped by Baxter's office this morning for a final discussion about his audit procedures. Explained why issues in London prevent a clean due diligence report. It's time for him to call Fullerton to discuss the pattern of suspicious last-minute sales. Baxter says his audit procedures followed standard practice. I should accept audit results and issue a clean report. Meeting with Fullerton is not necessary.

Called Fullerton's office and told his assistant I need to meet with him Friday morning in Camden to discuss a problem at Beta that prevents issuing a clean due diligence report.

Told Baxter his audit procedures are not acceptable. Disappointed he is not willing to report suspicious last-minute sales to Fullerton.

Amanda asks, "What do you think?"

"Michaud had a nose for smelling accounting problems but, I agree, I'm surprised his notes are so critical of a former colleague."

Amanda says, "I need to think about our next steps. Michaud's notes confirm Baxter lied to us. He knew why and when Michaud was meeting with Fullerton."

I say, "Let's take a break. It's almost eight and we can talk about this after dinner."

"Sure. Let's walk over to Coastal Prime. I need a break. This case is a puzzle."

47

We both have a restless night and Sunday dawns damp and foggy. I'm disappointed the chairs are too wet for breakfast on the aft deck.

Amanda says, "Damn. This foggy morning matches my gloomy outlook. These guys can all pay top defense lawyers. We face a lot of 'I don't recall' or quotes from the fifth amendment. I need some answers."

I say, "Let's solve this puzzle in steps. My investigation uncovered the accounting fraud. Miller, O'Donnell, and Baxter are all engaged in a coverup. You want to know who initiated and who facilitated the fraud."

Amanda says, "Right. Most fingers point at O'Donnell. If he didn't know, he should have known about the accounting fraud. All the fraudulent transactions passed through his accounting staff."

She smiles. "They're all pretending to cooperate so they can point fingers. O'Donnell's the logical place to start. I want Fullerton to arrange for O'Donnell to come to Portland."

# # #

Thirty minutes later, Amanda places a call from

Ruth on speaker.

"Hi, Amanda. Carson asked me to return your call. He said you want O'Donnell to come to Portland for a more official visit on Monday. What do you have in mind?"

"My earlier visits were helpful, but it's time to get everyone's statements documented. I want O'Donnell to appear voluntarily to answer some questions for the record. He's not being accused of a crime, but he's welcome to bring an attorney. The sooner we get this resolved, the sooner you can start new acquisition discussions with Tango."

Ruth says, "That's a powerful incentive. I'm sure Carson will tell O'Donnell to cooperate."

# # #

Ruth calls an hour later. "It's all arranged. O'Donnell will be at your office Monday afternoon."

"Thanks. Please schedule my next visit for Tuesday afternoon in Portland with Miller."

"You want Miller to come to Portland? I doubt he cooperates."

"Tell him it's best to cooperate with a voluntary visit if he has nothing to hide. He is free to bring his attorney. Miller has my card. He's welcome to call me if he has questions."

Ruth says, "I'll do my best."

I smile and ask, "Do you really think Miller will come to Portland?"

"Yes, but I expect him to object and have his assistant call me."

# # #

My phone flashes a call from *Degas* Sunday evening. I answer on speaker. "Anything more on Mike or Walt?"

"Maybe. Our consulting agreement with Alpha gives us access to all their systems until Fullerton terminates the agreement."

"Right, but I expected O'Donnell to block access once we submitted our report to Fullerton."

She says, "O'Donnell must be distracted. My workaround still works."

"Interesting oversight on O'Donnell's part. What have you learned?"

"Both Mike and Walt received bonuses from Beta's bonus pool the day after Mike had his encounter with Amanda."

"Humm .... Who authorized the payments?"

"O'Donnell."

"The brothers have disappeared." I ask, "Were those termination payments?"

"No. Their files say they are on vacation and both men are still on the payroll." She pauses.

"They haven't disappeared. Mike and Walt are in Las Vegas."

"How do you know?"

"They're both using their company credit cards. I can review their charges."

"Wow! Great work. Please post their charges to our secure site so we can monitor their whereabouts."

48

Portland, Maine

Amanda reviews information on her laptop while I drive to Portland Monday morning. She winks when her phone flashes a call. "It's Miller's office number."

"Good morning, this is Agent Amanda Smith."

"Yes, I understand Mr. Miller is a busy man and it would be more convenient for him to meet at his office. However, he needs to come to my office in Portland for this interview."

She smiles. "It'll be easier for Mr. Miller to eavesdrop if you place your phone on speaker."

She winks. "Oh, I thought I heard his voice in the background. Tell him innocent people don't resist cooperating with the FBI. I expect to see him at two o'clock on Tuesday. Goodbye."

I grin. "I can't wait to witness this session. You might need to 'bleep' some of his language. When are you going to confront Baxter? He lied to you about Michaud's last visit."

"I want to know what Miller has to hide before I confront Baxter."

# # #

When we arrive, Amanda arranges a camera on a tripod in a small conference room.

She examines the room. "This room with a view of the park is more informal than our interrogation room with that one-way mirror. I want O'Donnell to feel more relaxed than a suspect."

O'Donnell shows up promptly at two o'clock and says, "I arranged for one of our corporate attorneys to accompany me."

Amanda says, "No problem. I just want to get the information we discussed in Florida on our official record. We have coffee and soft drinks on the credenza. Just let me know if you want a break or need a private visit with your attorney. I appreciate your cooperation. I hope it's OK to have Steve sit in again."

O'Donnell says, "Sure. I'm happy to help. We need to get to the bottom of this. Let's get started."

The first hour with Amanda's questions is routine and O'Donnell drums his fingers on the table and yawns. Amanda stretches her arms and shoulders. "Let's take a ten-minute break."

Amanda resumes when O'Donnell returns. "Let's cover the circumstances of your bonus again for the record. Who authorized your bonus from Beta?"

"I told you, Fullerton."

"Who signed your bonus agreement?"

"Miller."

"Who told you Fullerton authorized your Beta bonus?"

"Miller."

She hands O'Donnell a document. "These are my notes from my interview with Miller."

O'Donnell's face turns crimson. "That bastard! He said Fullerton authorized my bonus from Beta. I just had to keep it a secret from Ruth."

Amanda hands him another document. "These are my notes from my interview with Fullerton."

"Damn. Miller lied to me."

Amanda returns the two documents to a small file and asks, "What was your reaction when Baxter told you Michaud would not issue a clean due diligence report?"

He pauses. "May I talk to my attorney?"

"Sure. Just step out of the room."

They return a few minutes later and O'Donnell's attorney says, "Please repeat the question."

"What was your reaction when Baxter told you Michaud would not issue a clean due diligence report?"

"I was shocked."

"Did you ask why?"

"Of course."

"What did Baxter tell you?"

"He said Michaud suspected a problem with sales in London."

"What did you do?"

"I called Miller."

"What did Miller say?"

"He was livid. He called Michaud a stupid green eyeshade auditor. Bragged about his sales team and told me to convince Michaud everything was accurate."

"What did you do?"

"I called Michaud."

"What happened?"

"He was on his flight to Maine. I left several messages. I asked him to share his concerns with me so we could address his questions before he discussed his concerns with Fullerton."

"Did he respond?"

"No. He didn't call that night. Brian Tucker told me Michaud had a boating accident the next morning."

"What happened next?"

He points to me. "Tango hired him for the due diligence project."

"Did you talk with Baxter or Miller after you left the message for Michaud?"

"Sure. I said I would keep them informed."

Amanda places a copy of my report on the table.

"Have you discussed the Paradox Report with Baxter?"

"Yes. I called Baxter after Fullerton's attorney sent me the report."

"What did he say?"

"He said his firm's attorney said it was best we didn't talk during an investigation."

"Have you discussed this investigation with Miller?"

He pauses. "I need another private minute with my attorney."

"Sure. We'll wait."

They return quickly and O'Donnell says, "It's not possible for me to have a rational conversation with Miller about this Paradox Report. You need to talk with Miller."

"Have you discussed this investigation with

Ruth?"

"Yes." He frowns. "Miller said I should convince Ruth that her investigation was unnecessary and a waste of money." He pauses. "I told Miller it was a waste of time. She speaks for Fullerton and he needs to call Fullerton if he wants her snooping to end."

"What happened?"

O'Donnell shrugs. "He lost his temper and told me to leave his office."

"When did you first learn about the suspicious transactions in London?"

"When Baxter called me. I was mistaken when I told you I learned about the transactions when Fullerton's attorneys sent me the report. I want to correct my statement."

Amanda smiles. "Thank you. Anything else you need to correct?"

"No."

"Have you discussed this investigation with Mike?"

"No. Why would I discuss it with Miller's driver?"

"Does Miller's driver participate in Beta's bonus pool?"

He ponders his answer. "Why is this relevant?"

"Why does Miller have a new driver?"

"He told me to get a substitute while his regular driver was on vacation."

"That's it for today. You've been very helpful."

# # #

Amanda says, "I prefer to have dinner at the apartment tonight, but there's nothing in my refrigerator. How's a pizza sound?"

"Sounds good to me. I'll call for delivery."

My phone flashes *Picasso* an hour later and I ask, "Anything new?"

"Beta paid five new agent commissions for one million each for fake sales shipped to the Dordrecht warehouse."

"When?"

"Last Wednesday. Two days after you handed our report to Fullerton."

"Who approved these commissions?"

"Miller authorized the manager of the London office to pay all sales commissions." She pauses. "I think the sales team paid themselves an exit bonus. I've posted copies of these payments on our secure site. A few more crumbs on the money trail leading to Beta's mysterious sales team."

49

The recording equipment is ready and Amanda is waiting at the conference room door for Miller's two o'clock interview. Miller and two men step off the elevator at two-twenty Tuesday afternoon.

Amanda smiles. "Good afternoon. I assume these gentlemen are your attorneys."

"Damn right. Let's get started. I'm busy, and this trip is an unnecessary expense for Beta."

Amanda looks to one of Miller's attorneys and taps her watch. "I prefer to start on time. You should tell your client it's not nice to keep the FBI waiting."

They enter the conference room and Miller looks at Amanda. "I want coffee."

She gestures. "Help yourself."

One of Miller's attorneys pours coffee and directs him to a seat in view of the camera. The attorneys take seats on either side and caution him to relax.

Miller points at me. "Why is he here?"

Amanda says, "I invited him. I'll be asking questions about the report his firm, Paradox-Research, prepared for Alpha."

Miller points to his watch and says, "Let's get started. You're wasting my time."

"Sure. I need to cover a few legal points, and I'm happy to answer questions from your attorneys."

Miller looks at the camera and combs his white hair. He squirms impatiently in his chair while Amanda covers her legal points and asks him a series of routine questions.

Amanda removes a document from her file. "I'm confused. When you arrived, you said today's trip was an unnecessary expense for Beta. Correct?"

"Damn right."

"Doesn't your employment agreement say Alpha pays all your expenses, including travel?"

"Absolutely. What about it?

"I'm confused. Which firm pays your expenses? Alpha or Beta?"

Miller glares at Amanda. "Alpha."

Miller's attorney taps him on the wrist and says, "It's important for your answers to be accurate."

Amanda nods her head and says, "Thank you."

She refers to her notes and asks, "What was your reaction when O'Donnell told you Baxter called him and Michaud wasn't planning to give you a clean due diligence report?"

"I took immediate action. I told O'Donnell to call

Michaud and fix the problem."

"What problem? Why wasn't Michaud giving you a clean report?"

"That stupid green eyeshade accountant was out of his league. I bet he never saw a company managed as efficiently as Beta."

"What was Michaud's problem with Beta?"

"That idiot was confused. He didn't understand our foreign sales program."

"What didn't he understand?"

"Something about commissions and product returns in London. Simple accounting stuff. I told O'Donnell to educate the fool."

"Were you concerned about Michaud's plan to meet with Fullerton?"

"Damn right. Beta is my responsibility. The damn fool should have come to me. I don't waste time. I take immediate action to solve problems."

"What happened next?"

"That stupid fool fell off his boat." Miller points to me. "Fullerton hired him."

Amanda says, "I'm confused. Didn't Tango hire his firm, Paradox-Research, to complete Michaud's due diligence?"

"That's right."

"So. What happened next?"

Miller pauses. "Fullerton got that damned woman involved in my deal."

"What woman?"

"That useless idiot, Ruth Simpson."

"Why?"

"Damned if I know. I had everything under control. Fullerton has no right to interfere in my business."

"What happened next?"

"Everything was going fine," he points at me, "until Fullerton hired him to investigate some accounting procedures in London." He stands. "Fullerton has no right to interfere in my business. That woman is dangerous. Managing Beta is my job!"

Miller's attorney taps his arm and motions for him to sit down in his chair.

Miller glares at his attorney. "Stop tapping my arm!"

"What happened next?"

"Fullerton's attorneys sent that damned report to us."

Amanda places a copy of my report on the table.

"That would be this Paradox Report, correct?"

"Yeah. I guess that's his report."

"What was your reaction to the report?"

"Fullerton had no right to have him do that so-called investigation. Managing Beta is my job."

"What was your reaction to the report?"

"I'm an incredibly tough and effective executive. I don't tolerate disloyalty. I took immediate action and fired the London sales team."

"Did you discuss the Paradox Report with anyone in London before you fired the sales team?"

He pauses. "Dealing directly with employment and accounting problems is O'Donnell's job."

"Who told the London sales team they were fired?"

"Damn it! Listen to me. I did."

"How?"

"I had my assistant email them a termination notice."

"When?"

"I told you. I don't tolerate disloyalty. I fired them immediately."

"When did you know the Paradox Report was accurate?"

Miller ponders his answer and his attorney asks, "May we have a private word with our client?"

"Sure."

They return a few minutes later, and Amanda repeats her question.

"When did you know the Paradox Report was accurate?"

"O'Donnell is responsible for the accuracy of Beta's accounting reports. I fired the London sales team for being disloyal to me."

Amanda pauses and looks at her notes. "Why was Michaud preparing a due diligence report?"

"That's a stupid question. Fullerton needs to sell Beta to Tango. Michaud was doing due diligence for Tango."

"Who benefits from the sale of Beta to Tango?"

He smirks. "Fullerton and O'Donnell."

"Don't you benefit?"

"You don't know much about acquisitions. I lose my job after the deal. I'll need to find a new job."

"Do you receive a bonus when Beta is sold?"

"Of course. That's standard practice."

"So, you also benefit. Correct?"

He smirks. "If you say so."

"Were you concerned about Baxter's call to O'Donnell about Michaud's report?"

"Of course. I told O'Donnell to fix it. I took

immediate action."

"What's the status of Beta's acquisition discussions today?"

Miller's face flushes. "I don't know. I'm not in the loop."

"Do you expect London's accounting problems to reduce Beta's sales price?"

"Listen. I achieved a phenomenal turnaround for Fullerton. The amazing sales growth I've generated created substantial value. I'd get a much higher price than that stupid woman if Fullerton had me conducting the negotiations."

Miller looks at his watch. "I'm busy, and this is a waste of my time. Let's wrap this up."

"Did you know about the potential accounting problems with the London sales team before you read the Paradox Report?"

"Damn it. I told you. I fired those guys immediately after reading that damned report."

"Humm .... Why didn't you take immediate action when you learned about Michaud's suspicions about your London sales team?"

"Damn it! I took immediate action. I told O'Donnell to fix it. Accounting is his job, not mine."

"Aren't you concerned about the accuracy of your sales reports?"

"I rely on O'Donnell to give me accurate financial

reports. The accuracy of Beta's financial reports is O'Donnell's job."

"What about Baxter?"

"Oh yeah. That fool screwed up too. I can't trust information from either of those fools."

"Have you discussed the Paradox Report with Baxter?"

"No. That's O'Donnell's job."

"Have you discussed the Paradox Report with O'Donnell?"

"Damn right. I told him to fix any problems."

"Have you discussed the Paradox Report with Ruth Simpson?"

"No. Why would I want to discuss it with that incompetent bitch?"

He turns to his attorney. "Stop tapping my arm. That woman is an incompetent bitch."

Amanda asks, "Have you discussed the Paradox Report with Fullerton?"

"Managing Beta is my job. My contract says he had no authority to interfere. I have nothing to say to him."

Amanda taps her watch. "We're getting close. I just have a few more questions."

Miller bristles. "It's about time."

Amanda smiles. "When was the last time you talked with Mike, your driver?"

"I don't recall. Probably the day before O'Donnell told me my driver went on vacation."

"When do you expect him back?"

Miller glares at Amanda. "What the hell does this have to do with accounting?"

"Does Beta pay Mike a bonus?"

"Damn it! O'Donnell is responsible for payroll and bonus payments."

"Have you discussed Michaud's death with Owen Clark, the investigator in Maine?"

"No. His accident has nothing to do with me."

"Did you know Michaud's death is being investigated as a homicide?"

"I think O'Donnell might have mentioned it."

"Do you think Michaud's death could be related to his due diligence findings?"

"That's a stupid question."

Amanda looks at Miller's attorneys. "I'm finished."

50

Amanda remains at the table to review documents and her notes while I take a walk. I stop at a nearby coffee shop and return with two lattes.

Amanda hands me her notepad. "I want to discuss this sequence of events with you before we drive back to Boothbay."

Thursday Morning: June 17

Michaud tells Baxter the sales discrepancies in London prevent issuing a clean due diligence report. Baxter's not willing to acknowledge London issue and meet with Fullerton. Michaud calls Fullerton's office and schedules a meeting with him in Camden to explain why he cannot issue a clean due diligence report.

Thursday Afternoon: June 17

Michaud on a flight to Portland/Drive to Boothbay.

Baxter calls O'Donnell to say Michaud is not issuing a clean due diligence report and plans to discuss London's sales problem with Fullerton on Friday.

O'Donnell calls Miller to report the call from Baxter and Michaud's plan to discuss London's sales with Fullerton. Miller tells O'Donnell to fix it.

Friday Morning: June 18

Michaud's body discovered floating in Boothbay Harbor.

She says, "All three men knew about Michaud's suspicions concering London's sales and his plan to meet with Fullerton on Friday, June 18th. All three were stonewalling your efforts to review customer transactions. This sure looks like a coordinated conspiracy to cover up the accounting fraud exposed by Michaud."

I conjecture. "Fullerton, Miller, and O'Donnell all resist disclosure of their activities. Baxter wants to retire without an accounting scandal happening on his last watch. Alpha doesn't have any audit functions. It's possible the London sales office was a rogue operation. Their results hit Miller's targets. Nobody wanted to ask questions."

Amanda says, "That's their problem. Michaud was asking questions. Baxter was supposed to ask questions. It's time I call Baxter and rock his boat."

"Mr. Baxter, this is Agent Smith with the FBI. I have a few more questions about Beta and appreciate your previous cooperation."

He says, "Glad to help."

"We've been doing our homework and gained access to Michaud's due diligence files. He was being stonewalled by O'Donnell and Miller. You had a meeting with him Thursday morning, June 17th, to discuss his concerns about Beta's sales in London. His notes say your audit was inadequate, and he scheduled his meeting with Fullerton on

Friday, June 18th. Is that correct?"

Baxter doesn't respond and Amanda continues.

"We also know you told O'Donnell that Michaud was concerned about London's sales and would not issue a clean due diligence report. As you know, the police have been investigating a link between Michaud's due diligence assignment and his death. You knew your friend planned to stay on his boat the night he was killed. I'm concerned about your safety as a potential witness and, if requested, the FBI can provide protection for you."

We hear Baxter stutter. "That's absurd. I don't need protection."

"Just be careful. Your friend is dead. Call me anytime."

Amanda says, "Let's go back to Boothbay. I think we've stirred the pot enough. It's time to return to the boat and wait for the judge to grant access to their phone and email records."

51

Boothbay Harbor, Maine

Amanda is beaming when I return from Shannon's with lobster rolls for lunch on Wednesday. "The judge granted my request for the past sixty days of cell phone records. He deferred action on my email request. He wants more evidence of a relationship between the accounting fraud and Michaud's death before he grants me an email fishing expedition."

I ask, "Where do you want to start?"

"Michaud's phone records confirm his call to Fullerton's office on Thursday. Let's start with the chain of events after Michaud meets with Baxter."

We pick up our laptops and I say, "I'll take Baxter, Ruth, and Fullerton."

An hour later, I say, "Baxter's calls to O'Donnell confirm O'Donnell's story. Baxter had no calls with Fullerton, Miller, Ruth, Walt, or Mike between the time of his meeting with Michaud and the time the body was discovered. What about O'Donnell?"

"O'Donnell's calls match his story. He called Michaud three times and left messages after talking with Baxter and Miller. No calls with Fullerton, Walt, or Mike. What about Ruth?"

Clark taps on my cabin top Wednesday evening. I open the cabin door and Amanda says, "Come in and take a seat."

She motions to the settee next to her and opens her laptop.

Clark says, "What's so important? I hope you finally linked that jerk Miller to my case. I can't wait to file extradition papers from Florida to Maine."

"Not exactly. I've summarized our investigation based on events, locations, and phone calls." She turns her laptop for Clark to read.

"I'll be damned. Fullerton's alibi for Walt doesn't hold water. Walt was in Boothbay."

Amanda says, "You won't need an extradition request. The men behind Michaud's death are on Fullerton's yacht in Camden."

52

Palm Beach, Florida

I witness a flurry of activity on Thursday as Amanda coordinates plans with Clark and agents in Las Vegas for Friday. Amanda and I catch the evening flight from Portland to Palm Beach.

# # #

Friday morning finds us in a rental car across the street from Beta's office building while we wait for Miller's arrival. Amanda checks with Clark to confirm today's activities.

"My agents in Las Vegas have Walt and Mike under surveillance. They are ready to move when I give them the signal. Are you in position?"

Clark says, "Yes. I'm with my team in Camden. Call me when Miller arrives."

Miller's Bentley arrives at nine, the driver escorts him to the door, and Miller walks into the building.

Amanda contacts Clark, her agents in Las Vegas, and the team standing by in Palm Beach. "We'll all move together at nine-twenty."

She's wearing her black FBI outfit today with large FBI lettering in gold on the back of her jacket. She flashes her FBI identification to the men at the security desk. "I'm Agent Smith with the FBI. Do not announce our arrival."

One agent remains in the lobby and I follow Amanda and two other agents into the elevator to the top floor. Amanda holds up her badge and motions for a startled receptionist to open the glass security door to Miller's executive suite.

Miller's assistant stands as we enter his office suite. "I'm sorry. Mr. Miller's busy and you don't have an appointment."

Amanda smiles. "You're mistaken. Mr. Miller has an appointment with us," and she opens the door to his office.

Miller is standing behind his desk. "What the hell is going on! Get out of my office!"

Amanda approaches his desk. "I'm Special Agent Amanda Smith with the FBI. I'm wearing my uniform today and you are being arrested for accounting fraud."

"Bullshit! Get out of my office!"

"Would you like to put on your suit coat before my agent places you in handcuffs?"

"What?" He sneers. "You can't handcuff me."

"Mr. Miller, you are under arrest. It's best if you remain silent and cooperate."

He shouts at his startled assistant standing inside his office doorway. "Call my lawyer!"

"You will have an opportunity to meet with your lawyer in our offices. Do you prefer to wear your suit coat, or should my agent place you in handcuffs now?"

He scowls. "I want to wear my suit coat."

The agent says, "That's good. Hands behind your back."

I step out of the doorway and watch Amanda and the agent escort Miller to an elevator. I wait to return to the lobby in the second elevator.

Amanda and the agents escort Miller to a large black SUV and join him for the drive to the FBI office. I walk across the street and follow in our rental car. I see a TV crew waiting as Amanda arrives at the FBI office with Miller.

# # #

I spend the next two hours at a nearby Starbucks waiting for Amanda to finish her paperwork. She sends a text at noon.

I'll meet you for lunch at E. R. Bradley's in an hour.

Amanda has her Cheshire Cat grin when she joins me at the table.

I say, "Worked like clockwork. I didn't know you tipped the news."

"We didn't. The crew said they received numerous anonymous calls from employees at Miller's office."

I laugh. "I watched the noon broadcast. 'Magic Max

Takes a Fall' was their lead story. What happened in Las Vegas?"

"Walt and his brother, Mike, were arrested at the hotel in Las Vegas. We're taking steps to extradite them to Maine."

"Have you talked with Clark?"

"Clark arrested Fullerton as an accessory to homicide this morning and he was booked at Clark's office in Augusta. Clark said the expression on Fullerton's face was priceless when his attorney asked why Walt was calling him for representation. The attorney posted bail and Fullerton was released after he surrendered his passport and agreed to remain in Maine."

"What about the accounting fraud?"

"Our agent arrested Fullerton when he left Clark's office and transported him to Portland. His attorney followed, and Fullerton will be out on bail tonight. A reporter from Portland and a TV crew were waiting for Fullerton's arrival."

She pauses. "I'll coordinate the case from Portland. I've booked our return on tonight's flight."

Epilogue

Boothbay Harbor, Maine

The leaves are turning bright orange in late September when we return to Boothbay Harbor Marina from our long-delayed vacation cruise to Northeast Harbor and Acadia. We stroll hand-in-hand across the footbridge for dinner at Coastal Prime. I order a bottle of Champagne and toast, "To another case successfully prosecuted."

Amanda smiles. "Thanks. I'm glad it's over. Miller's attempts to blame O'Donnell backfired when O'Donnell agreed to cooperate with our attorneys. He said Miller knew about the illegal payoffs to government officials from the beginning. Miller's attorney was speechless when Miller said, 'Damn it! Why pick on me? Everybody does it'."

I say, "O'Donnell testified he warned Miller about possible fake sales when the audit team started asking questions."

Amanda frowns. "Miller responded by eliminating Beta's audit team and O'Donnell stopped asking questions after he was added to Beta's bonus pool. Miller sent Mike to confront Ruth and you when you started asking questions."

I ask, "Why do you think Baxter didn't question London's sales activity?"

"I don't know. Baxter helped facilitate the fraud when he reduced fieldwork in London after Miller reduced the audit fee. However, we found no evidence he was aware of the accounting fraud and dropped charges. Alpha's investors are suing the accounting firm and Baxter is being forced into early retirement."

I sigh. "I was disappointed when we couldn't link Fullerton to the fraud and you had to drop charges."

Amanda shrugs. "Fullerton needed to sell Beta to restore his reputation as a successful investor. He didn't want to question Miller's results. His actions to avoid hearing bad news led to Michaud's death."

"I was pleased Clark sent you flowers after the judge accepted pleas from Fullerton and Walt."

Amanda shakes her head. "What a sad story of unintended consequences. Ruth was in Arizona, so Fullerton sent Walt to convince Michaud to return to Palm Beach and talk to O'Donnell."

I say, "Clark got a break when forensics matched Walt's wetsuit with evidence on the sailboat."

Amanda frowns. "Stupid plan. Walt said he planned to use his special forces training to scare Michaud into cooperating. So, he changed into his wetsuit and swam to Michaud's sailboat. He claimed Michaud's death was an accident and agreed to plead guilty to unintentional homicide. Walt's testimony implicated Fullerton as an accessory."

She pauses. "Michaud's dead and their plea deals don't feel like adequate punishment. But it's the best the attorneys could do."

Amanda shakes her head. "Miller's abusive style didn't win him any loyalty. He encouraged fraud by rewarding large bonuses to hit unreasonable sales goals and he demanded higher sales every quarter. Once the fraud started, there was no way to unwind it without selling Beta."

I grin. "Tango completed the acquisition of Beta a week ago. London's fraudulent accounts were eliminated, but Ruth negotiated a fair price for Beta after sharing her recommendations with Parker. Beta's investors recognized a substantial gain and Alpha's board hired her to sell Alpha's other investments."

Amanda smiles. "Ruth's a tough negotiator. I was pleased to learn her bonus for selling Beta was the same amount Miller would have received."

I shake my head. "It's tragic. Michaud's dead because Fullerton and Miller didn't want to be embarrassed by failure. Ruth's sale of Beta was a financial success. Their egos were their downfall."

We stop on the footbridge on our way back to Kim's marina to admire the moon's reflection across Boothbay Harbor. Amanda smiles. "I'm sad our wonderful two-week cruise Downeast to Acadia is over, but it's nice to be back in Boothbay for our last night. I'm glad tomorrow's forecast is for calm seas on your voyage up Penobscot Bay to Belfast."

I squeeze her hand and pull her toward me for a kiss.

Death & Due Diligence

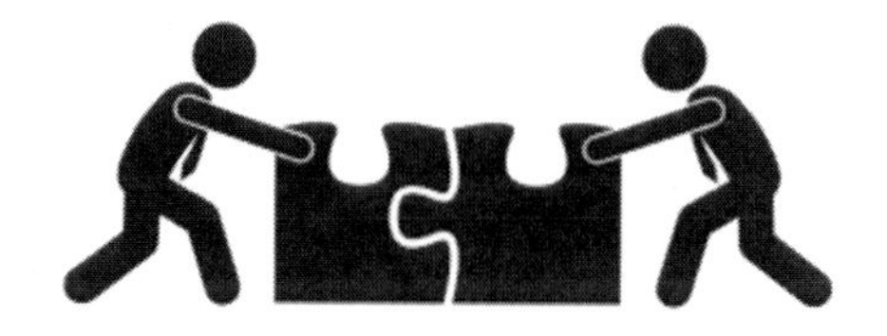

Paradox Murder Mystery Series

Join Steve and Amanda as they embark on another 'stand-alone' murder investigation

2022 Death & Due Diligence

2021 Prospère Puzzle

2020 Paris Connection

2020 Synthetic Escape

2019 Deadly Curiosity

2019 Turquoise Deception

2018 Death Trap

About the Author

Charles and his wife, Molly, and their dog, Scupper, enjoy cruising Penobscot Bay and the coast of Maine aboard their Duffy 37, a Maine-built lobster boat with a custom interior.

Charles enjoyed a fifty-year career in the banking industry having served as an executive officer and as a board member of several banking institutions. His Paradox Murder Mystery series blends his financial experience with his love of cruising.

Additional information is available at:

www.Paradox-Research.com

Paradox09A@Gmail.com

Appreciation

Molly

Alison, Amy, David, Linda, Martha, Robert

Special Thanks To

Kim, Jeff, and Dan

for being part of the story

Acknowledgments

Our summer cruises along the coast of Maine provide extensive information and insight about the locations described in Death & Due Diligence.

I am very grateful to the following:

Boothbay Harbor Marina

Front Street Shipyard

Lyman-Morse Camden

Photos

Molly Potter Thayer

Books by Charles J Thayer

Non-Fiction

2021 It Is What It Is [2nd Edition]

Saving American West Bank

2017 Bank Director Survival Guide

Practical Guide for Bank Board Members

2016 Credit Check

Giving Credit Where Credit Is Due

2010 It Is What It Is

Saving American West Bank

1986 The Bank Director's Handbook

Auburn House: 2nd Edition
Chapter: Asset/Liability Management

1983 Bankers Desk Reference

Warren, Gorham & Lamont
Chapter: Financial Futures Market

1981 The Bank Director's Handbook

Auburn House: 1st Edition
Chapter: Asset/Liability Management

Made in United States
North Haven, CT
16 May 2022